# LOSING OUR EDGE

# LOSING OUR EDGE

*a novel*

## JEFF GOMEZ

Copyright © 2018 by Jeff Gomez

www.dontcallhome.com

978-1-5040-0950-8

Distributed in 2018 by Open Road Distribution
180 Maiden Lane
New York, NY 10038
www.openroadmedia.com

# CONTENTS

# LOSING OUR EDGE

It's all fine to say, "Time will heal everything, this too shall pass away. People will forget"—and things like that when you are not involved, but when you are there is no passage of time, people do not forget and you are in the middle of something that does not change.

—John Steinbeck
*Cannery Row*

# 1: WE ARE BACK

"Dad."

His father's standing on the front porch of the home where Mark grew up. His family moved here when he was almost eight, and when Mark turned nineteen he moved into an apartment just across town, skipping college so he could write songs and tour with his band. The name PELLION still remains in fancy script on a porcelain plaque above the mailbox. He remembers when his parents added it, the day they moved in. They were so proud to move from one side of Kitty to the other. So happy that they now lived in Tiger Bay, the Nice Part of Town. Even though Mark sees his parents every Christmas at their house in the mountains of North Carolina—he drives down from Manhattan; they drive down from Virginia—this is the first time in twenty years he's been home.

"Dad," he repeats. "It's late. You didn't have to wait up."

It's almost midnight, all the windows along the suburban street are dark—except for the warm glow coming from behind the closed curtains of his parents' living room.

"Couldn't sleep," his dad says. There's a smile on his face. "You made it."

Mark grabs a duffel bag from the back seat, locks the rental car, and walks up the front steps. He leans in for a hug.

"How's Mom?"

"Good. She's asleep, but she's excited to see you, too."

Mark pulls back.

"Sorry. I got a later start than I meant to. And there was traffic."

His dad looks down at the ground and nods, running a slipper over the weathered welcome mat—so worn away, the letters are just ghosts.

"It's so—it's good to have you home."

They go inside. Mark places the duffel bag on the floor in the hallway and walks into the living room. It's exactly as he remembers it—same pictures, same wallpaper, same carpet. The only thing different is a new flat-screen TV and cable box glowing in the corner. Under the TV is the same VCR they bought when he was in high school.

"How was the drive?"

"Long. My back's killing me."

When neither of them speaks again, there's silence. It startles Mark. New York City doesn't do quiet. His dad finally says, "We've been getting phone calls."

"Why? About what?"

His dad walks to where an old Dell laptop is open on top of an ottoman. The ottoman is faded and threadbare in two spots from where Mark's dad likes to put up his feet to watch TV. Mark sits on the couch—the only couch he can remember his parents ever owning—and looks at the computer. He sees his face. It's a picture of him from the nineties, an old publicity shot for his band Bottlecap from when they were on that first record label, the one their friend Dave ran. Gary and Steve are on either side of him. All three of them are wearing flannel shirts and sitting in a field located on the outskirts of town—if Mark remembers correctly—almost all the way to Mechanicsville. Next to the photo is a *Kitty Courier* story about the show next week.

## BOTTLECAP, OTHERS TO UNITE FOR BENEFIT

On May 18th Kitty legends Bottlecap, the band who had a minor hit at the tail end of the grunge years with their single "I Want to Feel You," will reform for one night as part of a benefit for local company VR Records.

Label owner and founder Dave Rowland says, "It means the world to me that all of my old groups, and my old friends, are getting back together to help me save VR Records. They helped put it on the map all those years ago, and I hope they can help me keep it going now."

VR, which shortened its name from Violent Revolution soon after the 9/11 terrorist attacks, is run out of Rowland's home and now releases music digitally. Its last vinyl record was released in 2002, and its last CD was released in 2010.

The original members of Bottlecap haven't played together since their original singer and Kitty native Mark Pellion stormed out of the Los Angeles recording sessions for their major label debut twenty years ago. Pellion will be joined by bassist Gary Reiger and drummer Steve Haverkamp, both of whom have moved back to Kitty since Bottlecap called it quits in 2001. Steve is now a salesman at Haverkamp Motors, while Gary still plays in a variety of local bands.

Bottlecap will be joined by other bands under the VR label, including the Disappointed and the Deer Park, though neither group has played in Kitty since local nightclub the Scene closed its doors in 1998.

The concert will be held at the Dark Star Lounge next Saturday at 8:00 PM. Advance tickets are available online or at the Dark Star box office during regular business hours.

When Mark's done reading, he looks up and sees his dad watching him, smiling. There's not a lot of light in the room—just what's coming from the hallway and the kitchen—but what light there is gets caught in his dad's eyes. It's been a long time since Mark's seen him look like this.

"The Nearys called. Do you remember the Nearys, Mark?"

"Who? No. But that's—I didn't think it'd be such a big deal."

"You forget how small this town is, Mark. It's not," the old man laughs, "Manhattan."

Mark closes the computer. Without the glowing screen, the room is just shadows.

"Anyway, you must be tired. You need help with your luggage?"

Mark gets up, grabs the duffel bag.

"Tomorrow. Traveling light for now."

Mark moves toward the stairs. He can see his dad's about to say something. Mark pauses, waiting for him to speak.

"Laura still lives here, you know."

"I know, Dad."

Mark didn't know, not for sure, but he figured.

"I just thought you'd want to—anyway, you go on to bed. I'll lock up down here."

"Thanks, Dad."

Mark walks quietly up the dark staircase. At the top, he can hear his mom breathing at the end of the hallway. Downstairs he hears his dad turning off lights and then walking through the kitchen to check the back door, the nightly routine hasn't changed after all these years. His steps are heavy, plodding. It sounds like he's carrying suitcases, but all he's carrying is himself. Mark tries to remember how old his parents are, but can't.

*Sixties? Seventies?*

Every year when they get together in December, Mark notices a decline in their health. They're always a bit slower than the year before. His dad keeps getting thinner, and his hands shake, while his mom seems to shrink all over. Walking into the house tonight, he was depressed to discover it no longer smelled like his parents. Now it just smells like old people.

Mark enters his room, not bothering to turn on the light. He slips off his shoes, takes off his pants, and climbs into bed. He can't remember a time growing up that he didn't sleep in this bed. It may even be the bed he's had since leaving the crib. When he was a boy, the bed seemed huge. He would pretend it was a train, a boat, a plane coasting through the sky. Now it's just a bed. He pulls the covers over himself and smells dust, some of which must be made of him. Mark closes his eyes and tries to sleep.

Charles is sure he smells mold. He's positive. He can practically see it floating in the air, green clouds of evil. Acrid, acidy, eating away at his brain. With every breath, he feels his intelligence dip.

"Darling, stop sniffing."

His wife, Grace, enters the room, carrying a cup of coffee. Charles is in bed, his Ralph Lauren pajamas wrinkled from tossing and turning all night. He's staring at the ceiling, nostrils opening and closing. Grace is wearing workout pants, a Lululemon sweatshirt, and bright purple New Balance sneakers.

She hands Charles the coffee. On the mug are pictures of their daughter, Maddie. The photos—Charles holding Maddie, Maddie yawning, Maddie sleeping in a stroller—are faded. The mug was a gift from Grace to Charles on his first Father's Day. Maddie was just five months old at the time. She turned eight three weeks ago, and Charles is freaking out.

Last month he noticed stains on the ceiling of her room. When he went into the attic to investigate, he found puddles of water on the insulation and dark streaks on the boards that formed the underside of the roof frame. Apparently the roof had been leaking for years despite having been replaced shortly before Charles and Grace bought the house five years ago.

The problem was that the flashing hadn't been installed properly. There were also leaks at the joints between the roof and the chimney, as well as between the sloped sections at the front of the roof. Rain had leaked down to the rafters, resulting in wood rot and mold. Not that he liked the idea of rotting wood, but the mold is what scared Charles the most. The bedrooms were on the second floor, with Maddie's room sitting right underneath the worst of the damage.

"You can't smell the mold, remember?" Now Grace is staring at the ceiling, too. "That's what makes it so dangerous. One of the contractors told us that."

Last weekend Charles had three different contractors come out and take a look, and they all said the same thing. The whole roof needed to be replaced. What pissed off Charles the most was that if the leaks had been caught earlier it would have been a simple repair. Just a few hundred bucks. When the contractors gave their estimates for the work, Charles couldn't believe it. The price ranged from twenty to thirty thousand dollars. For a fucking roof.

Charles finally looks away from the ceiling and takes a sip of the coffee. It's hot and strong. He takes another sip and then trades the coffee for the MacBook that's sitting on his nightstand.

"Sweetheart, what are you doing?" Grace's arms are crossed. "You know the rule. No laptops in bed."

"I know, I know," Charles says as he enters his password. "I just want to check my email really quick before heading to the office."

Grace stomps out of the room. She enters the bathroom that's right outside the bedroom. Charles hears the faucet go on and off. Drawers are opened and closed.

Charles clicks on the Outlook icon, waits impatiently for it to load. There have been some rumors that his department's going to be reorganized and that O'Brien, the head of their branch, is looking to promote someone to vice president. Charles and a couple of other guys on his floor—Dylan and Brooks—have been speculating about who's going to get the job. Charles was hoping for an email from one of them with some news or gossip. But there's nothing.

Frustrated, Charles clicks over to Gmail. The first thing he sees is from the local paper, the *Kitty Courier*. Sometimes, if there's something newsworthy, they'll send out an email with a link to the story. Usually it's just about ice storms or dates of the county fair, nothing that ever interests Charles. But this headline reads BOTTLECAP, OTHERS TO UNITE FOR BENEFIT. He quickly scans the article.

"No way!" he calls out. "Honey, you've got to see this."

Grace comes back into the room.

"What is it?"

"Bottlecap, this band from town I used to love, is getting back together. They're playing a show next week."

"Bottlecap?" she says, as she puts her hair into a ponytail, "Never heard of them."

"That's what you get for growing up in Crozet. Here in Kitty they were a legend."

"Legend?" She sounds skeptical.

"Legend," he repeats, before adding, "well, to me and friends anyway. Maybe I'll see if Randy wants to go."

"That guy you used to live with?"

Grace has never met him but Charles is always telling stories about Randy, about how crazy their life was in the nineties, how they were both really into the music scene in town, and how they tried to get a zine off the ground. This was right after college, when everyone still called Charles by his childhood nickname "Chipp."

"Those were great days."

Even though Charles says this under his breath, Grace hears him. She smiles and says, "These days are pretty great, too. Don't you think? Speaking of which, can you drop off Maddie at school on your way in to work? I'd like to make an early yoga class."

Charles shakes his head.

"Can't, sweetie, sorry. There's that big meeting today, remember? O'Brien's delivering our quarterly results. 'Attendance is mandatory.'"

"Yeah, but you said that's not until noon."

Charles shrugs.

"It isn't, but it's a big day. I need to get there early. Show I'm a team player." He looks toward his closet. "Should probably wear a tie, too. Just in case."

"Okay, fine," Grace says, "but you owe me. Can you take Grace to the dentist on Thursday? I've got Pilates."

"Deal," Charles says as he writes a quick email to Randy, asking for forgiveness for being out of touch, and seeing if he wants to get together soon. He finishes the email and hits SEND.

Grace says, "Where did he end up, anyway?"

"Who?"

"Randy, your old friend."

Charles looks out the window, considering this.

"I don't know. It's been so long since I've seen him—eight, ten years, maybe." He finally gets out of bed. "But Randy was a sharp guy. I'm sure he landed on his feet."

◎◎◎

Randy slept in his clothes again. He doesn't know why. He can't remember anything from the night before. All he knows is that there's sunlight pouring into his room, he's waking up, and he's still wearing the jeans and T-shirt from yesterday. All that comes back to him is a girl and a bottle and his car that he should not have driven home from wherever he had been.

*Shit, what time is it? I'm going to be late for my shift.*

He sits up and looks for the clock, but can't find it. He knows there's one in his room somewhere. It's digital and he hears it beep occasionally, some long forgotten alarm going off. Some prior version of him late for something. But there's too much clutter to find it. Dirty clothes, unwashed dishes, and empty packets of cigarettes are everywhere.

He buries his head under a pillow, tries to go back to sleep, tries to escape the day he's not yet ready to face. But noises coming from the kitchen make his headache grow even larger. It's that shitty electronic music Cody and Hunter are always playing. There's not even a stereo in the apartment. His roommates just "stream" music on their laptops from wherever they happen to be sitting.

Randy used to live alone. But over the past decade his rent kept going up while his pay stayed the same and, as a result, he had to move into smaller and smaller apartments. He finally couldn't afford to live on his own. So he has roommates again, both younger than him by decades. If they were amused when Randy first showed up and told them he'd come about the Craigslist ad, they were downright baffled when he said he'd take it—it was the smallest room in the house. Randy, forty-four and old enough to be their father, knew they didn't want him there. But what could they say? He moved in before they could think of an excuse.

Randy gets out of bed, his head throbbing and his back aching. He tries to stand up straight but can't. Hunched over, he rummages around his desk piled high with junk—cans of soda, crumpled receipts, unopened mail. Most of the mail is bills, most of them marked PAST DUE. He finally finds his cell phone, an old BlackBerry with a keyboard instead of a touch screen (no one has these anymore) and discovers it's almost ten. Since his shift at Bookstorage starts at one, he usually wakes up around noon. From 1:00 PM until closing, four days a week. That's his schedule.

He clears away a bunch of dirty clothes from a cheap-looking chair in front of an Ikea desk that's covered in stickers, and sits down. He picks up two socks from the floor that seem clean and appear to match. He puts them on and looks down at the jeans and T-shirt he slept in. They seem okay. He reaches for a pair of Doc Martens he's had forever. The orange stitching around the soles turned black long ago. As he bends over to lace them up, his knees crack. When he stands, he hears something pop. He grabs his wallet, a pack of cigarettes, and his car keys from a plastic cereal bowl atop a cluttered dresser.

He enters the shared area of the house and sees Cody and Hunter sitting at opposite ends of the kitchen table—chairs leaned back, computers on their laps, feet on the table. Cody is tall, angular, with jet-black hair in an '80s new-wave style. Hunter's shorter, stockier and soft, with hair that looks like it's never seen scissors and yet is still, somehow, stylish. They're both coders. Freelance. That typing they're doing right now, that's their work. One of them does something with databases and the other builds system architecture, whatever that is.

"You didn't buy free-trade coffee again," Cody says. He doesn't look up when he speaks. He just keeps typing on a laptop covered with stickers. *Tumblr. Seatr. Pillw.* The music coming out of Cody's laptop consists of beeps and glitches layered over a skittering beat that sounds like it's underwater. Randy listens for guitar or bass or vocals but doesn't hear them. Similar but different music is coming out of Hunter's laptop a few feet away. "Coffee's the one thing we all share. You *know* I only drink free-trade coffee."

"I bought coffee," Randy says. "I bought Yuban."

"Yuban is *not* free-trade," Hunter says. "It's barely even coffee."

"What's the difference?" Randy says. "As long as it's hot and brown and has caffeine, it's coffee."

Randy walks to the pantry to get something for breakfast, but stops since he knows there's nothing inside that's his. As he stands there, he hears Cody mutter something under his breath. His voice is too low for Randy to hear clearly, so he only picks up random words instead. *Indigenous. Carbon footprint. Agave.*

"And you threw out all of my quinoa," Hunter says.

Randy turns to face him.

"That brown stuff that was in the fridge? I thought it was rice that had gone bad."

Cody says to Hunter, "I'm just glad they finally opened a Whole Foods in Kitty. Try getting anything organic at the Food Lion."

Hunter says to Cody, "That's like shopping in a Third World country. Trans fat galore and everything's in a box with a cartoon character on it."

"I don't know what it is with you two," Randy says. "Would it kill you to eat a Pop Tart?"

Cody says, "Eventually, yes."

Randy goes to the fridge, opens it. There's nothing inside that's his.

"You eat all this micro-organic local shit, and yet you drink Pabst Blue Ribbon. What's that all about?"

"It's ironic."

"It's shit."

"Jesus, Randy," Hunter says. "It can be both."

Randy slams the fridge shut. Inside, bottles of an all-juice cleanse belonging to Hunter knock together to make a sound like what's coming out of their laptops.

Cody says, "You're also late with the rent again."

"I know."

"You've been late every month for almost six months—"

"I *know.*"

"—and I keep having to remind you."

Even though he's talking to Randy, Cody's eyes are fixed on his screen, and his fingers never stop moving across the keyboard.

"Look, we all knew this was a weird situation when you moved in, what with you being . . . you know."

They can't even bring themselves to say the word. As if it were a virus they could catch.

"Old, you mean?" Randy says. "What with me being *old*? Is *that* what you're trying to say?"

Cody refuses to take the bait. He continues in an even voice.

"The lease is in my name, Randy. If the landlord wanted to be a dick he could kick us all out, and that would ruin my credit rating."

"Credit rating? When I was your age I never worried about my goddamn credit rating."

Cody stops typing. He finally focuses on Randy.

"And now look where you are."

Randy stomps out of the house, slamming the door behind him. From the sidewalk, he can hear Cody and Hunter laughing. He turns to where his rust-covered '97 Tercel is parked on the street, sandwiched between Cody's all-black GTI and Hunter's bright-blue Honda Hybrid.

*They both have better cars than I do. How is that possible? They're just kids.*

Randy gets in the car. His head feels like it's on fire and his stomach is doing somersaults. He needs food and coffee, but first he has to check his email. On days when he goes to work, Bill, his boss, will sometimes email him, telling him to come in late, or early, or not at all. Usually Randy hopes to be given the day off due to it being a slow day or double scheduling. But with less than a hundred dollars in his checking account, nothing in savings, and payday two weeks away, Randy prays for that not to happen today.

There's nothing from Bill, but he's surprised to see an email from Charles, an old friend of his. The guy he lived with after they both got kicked out of college.

Randy reaches for the cigarettes in his pocket. He lights one using the Bic lighter he keeps in the drink holder between the two front seats, the dashboard lighter having stopped working long ago.

"Corporate jackass," he says out loud. Randy takes a deep drag, exhaling through his nose. "He's probably in a meeting right now."

Someone took all the erasers. Craig stands at a whiteboard, the big one in the conference room. He has a red marker in his hand, his back is to the room, and for the last twenty minutes he's been outlining his user acquisition strategy for Q4. One side of the whiteboard is filled with boxes that have words in them like PAID, GROWTH, ORGANIC, and CHURN. The other side has circles with dollar amounts and percentages. Arrows in different colors run from one set of boxes to the other. Craig now writes out his slogan for the fall marketing campaign that's going to culminate in a big holiday push. LET SEATR BE YOUR SLEIGH THIS CHRISTMAS. He then adds SEATR—WE GET YOU THERE.

Seatr is a website that's supposed to let users buy and resell airline tickets, but—even though they're live and getting traffic—the site doesn't allow anyone to actually purchase anything. So, technically, Seatr's *not* getting you there. But everyone at the company's trying to ignore that.

He writes SOCIAL and then MOBILE and then stops. There's no room to write LOCAL. Craig has run out of space.

He turns around and sees Josh—Seatr's CEO and Craig's boss—and the other members of the board squirming uneasily in their chairs. Josh, at twenty-six, is already a millionaire. A few years ago he sold his first company to Microsoft.

*I'm losing them.*

Craig quickly erases a few bullet points with the heel of his palm, leaving a red smear, and writes LOCAL. As he describes to the board his three-tier consumer value proposition, he's careful not to put his hands in his pockets. He doesn't want to get red ink on his designer jeans. The jeans cost $200. He doesn't know why. They don't seem any different than the $40 Levi's he can buy at the mall. But three of Seatr's board members wear this brand, so he figured he had better wear them, too.

Craig is about to detail his strategy for search engine optimization when Josh interrupts him.

"This is all awesome stuff, Craig. *Awesome.*"

The board members, including the co-founder of Josh's previous company, advisors from other local startups, and the angel investor who supplied most of the first-round seed money to get Seatr started all nod and repeat, "Awesome."

"The problem," Josh says, "is that we're live *now*. We need to start getting users. Quarterly projections and plans for the holidays are all well and good, but we need people *today.*"

"Yeah, but the site's not even working properly," Craig says. "Our database is too slow, the user interface is confusing, and transactions are failing because of—"

Josh shakes his head from side to side.

"Craig, Craig, Craig, I hear you. I *hear* you. And I love what you've done." He waves at the whiteboard. "I just need you to rethink all of this so that we get users *now*, not in the fall. Okay? 'Get Big Fast.' *That's* our slogan."

"Actually, that was Amazon's slogan."

"And look what it did for them," Josh says. "Sixty-one billion in sales last year. Not too shabby."

Once again the board members nod their heads in unison, whispering under their collective breath, "Billions." On the table is an assortment of Sigg bottles, Nalgene bottles, cans of Red Bull, Hint water, even a beer. That's it. No notebooks, no pads of paper. No one's writing anything down. Only Josh, with his open laptop, seems to be paying much attention.

At forty-five, Craig is considerably older than anyone else at Seatr. The next closest person in age is a thirty-one-year-old coder whom all the other coders call Granddad. Behind his back, Craig's known as Grandpa Moses. Even Granddad makes jokes about how old Craig is. His last job was at a PR firm in Charlottesville. He'd worked there for ten years and—even though it paid well—the long hours and exhausting commute finally became too much to handle. So he started looking for a new job. When a friend told him about Seatr, it seemed like a good time to try something new. That was seven months ago.

It was liberating at first, freeing himself from all the corporate bullshit he'd endured for so long. Craig enjoyed taking it easy, drinking beer while he worked, and having meetings on the roof or the patch of grass downstairs. Josh was a good kid and maybe he was on to something. Maybe Seatr would be a success and they'd all be rich. Or maybe they'd pivot to something else and *that* would be the thing that would make them rich. The world was full of billionaires who'd done less. But lately it'd been a drag. Craig's not sure how Seatr is supposed to actually make money, and he's tired of always being the oldest person in the room. The coders laughed at him for not knowing how to run an SQL query. And even though Josh tried to be patient during their one-on-ones, Craig had begun to sense some tension. And now he's in a conference room, standing in front of a whiteboard, holding a red marker, and someone took all the erasers.

Craig just sits down, not knowing what else to say.

"Now," Josh says, sounding exhausted. "What's next on the agenda?"

While the head of product gives an update about the redesign of the Android app, Craig—bored, deflated—opens his laptop and checks his email. He scrolls through his inbox and sees an email alert from the *Kitty Courier*. The story's about the band Bottlecap getting back together for a concert. Craig saw Bottlecap live a bunch of times when he was younger. He even used to have their records; although, since his divorce, most of that stuff's in storage and hasn't been listened to in years. He tries to calculate, to do the math.

*That was twenty years ago.*

Mismatched furniture. McJobs. Getting so drunk on Tuesday you still had a buzz when you woke up on Wednesday.

*Ashley.*

The girl he'd met in college and lived with for years until it finally imploded after Charlottesville. The first girl he'd ever been really serious about. The girl his parents had met and loved.

*Ashley.*

"Craig?"

He looks up. Josh and the board are staring at him.

"Meeting's over, dude." Josh stands up. "Want to join us for sushi?"

"Uh, no—no," Craig says. He's still thinking of her. "I'll stick around and work on these sales projections."

Josh nods, bows at the waist, and says, "*Namaste.*" Everyone but Craig files out of the room. He turns back to his laptop, muttering.

*Ashley. Ashley. Ashley.*

Margot has come by to show off her new baby, and even though there's not enough room everyone has squeezed into Ashley's office. Ashley and Margot shared an office during the first two years they worked together—a different office, not the small one Ashley now has—so she was the first person Margot wanted to see. Margot was the last person Ashley wanted to see. It's bad enough that most of the women she works with have kids, so to now have Margot coming by flaunting her baby while the whole company—even the receptionist is there— squeezes into her office, feels like too much.

Lucy is three months old, her skin creamy smooth, and her head covered in wispy blond hair. As Margot takes her out of the Baby Bjorn, Lucy drools and makes bubbles out of her spit. Margot places her in the center of Ashley's desk. Lucy is dressed in a pink Janie and Jack outfit that's color-coordinated with the ribbon that's stretched around her head. She knocks over a cup filled with pencils and pens. Everyone thinks this is adorable.

"Look at those muscles!"

"She's going to play soccer!"

"How're you sleeping?"

"Is Zach pitching in?"

Ashley thinks back to when Margot first got the job. Margot hadn't even met Zach yet. She remembers the Monday after they had their first date—they were set up by mutual friends—when Margot went on and on about how handsome and sensitive Zach was. She was sure that he was "the one." Ashley, having heard this a few times already, was cynical and counseled caution. And now, three years later, Margot's in Ashley's smaller office with her newborn baby and is beaming.

"She looks just like you!"

"What a face. What a *face!*"

"And just look at that smile!"

"And so much hair!"

"Ashley, you *have* to hold her."

Ashley looks up after hearing her name. She's not even sure who said it. When a baby's around, all women's voices sound the same.

Before she can answer, much less make up some excuse (*I have a cold, I'm contagious, I have polio, don't touch me*), the little girl is placed into Ashley's arms. Ashley doesn't know what to do.

"It's just a *baby*, Ashley," someone says. "She's not going to bite."

Margot says, "Want to bet?" and the whole office explodes with laughter.

Ashley juggles Lucy more than holds her. She brings the baby to one shoulder and then the other, before trading her for the crook of her left arm and then the right. Finally, she just grabs Lucy under her shoulders and holds the baby up to the fluorescent lights of the office, like in that Disney movie, until someone else takes Lucy.

Ashley is just about to make up some excuse to slip out of the office when her boss, Deborah, suddenly joins the group. For some reason this elicits a new round of *oohing* and *ahhing* over the baby.

"Those eyes! I just can't get over her eyes."

"Such small hands."

"The cleft chin she must get from her father."

"*Turnadot*," Ashley tries to break in. "Anyone ever see *Turnadot*? Andrew and I saw it last month in Arlington. Amazing soprano, let me tell you."

Margot points to the baby. "You want to hear a pair of lungs? You should see this one when she's hungry."

More laughter, Ashley's attempt to change the subject fizzles into yet another round of questions about the baby's sleeping patterns, how long Margot was in labor, and whether or not they're going to send Lucy to private school. When Margot pulls out her breast and starts feeding the baby, Ashley has to look away. She's staring at the floor when Bea announces that the food has just arrived and lunch is being served in the break room.

Everyone finally leaves Ashley's office. Everyone except a young woman named Sherry who's new and works the front desk. Ashley's not sure why Sherry's still here, but she wishes she'd leave.

Ashley catches Sherry's glance at her wedding ring. She says, "You and your husband have any kids?"

Ashley stiffens.

"Us? No, we just—no."

"Well, you should. You really should. They're a joy. *Such* a joy."

"Joy, yes. Look, Sherry, I really have to—"

"My fiancé and I are planning on having a *large* family. A large family. We both come from large families."

"Fiancé?"

Ashley notices Sherry's ring. It's huge. Little diamonds surrounding one big diamond. When Sherry sees Ashley looking at the ring, she looks at it, too.

"Can you *believe* it? He proposed two weeks ago. I'm going to be a June bride. *Next* June, of course. We're going to be married on Hilton Head. His family has a house there." Sherry looks from the ring to Ashley.

"How about you? Where'd you get married?"

"City Hall," Ashley says. She stands up. "Will you excuse me? I have to go grab—I want to get a salad."

Sherry looks toward the break room. The voices of the women carry down the hall, with Lucy's howling added to the mix.

"But Deborah ordered food. Bea just said. We *have* salad."

Grabbing her bag, Ashley says, "I just need a little air."

She exits the office. Not wanting to wait for the elevator, she takes the stairs two at a time. Twice she almost trips in her heels. Outside, the cool air is a balm on her flushed cheeks. She puts a hand to her forehead and feels sweat. She tries to breathe calmly, but it's difficult.

Ashley reaches into her purse for a prescription bottle. She removes the cap—she's an expert at doing this with only one hand, even on the childproof kind—and brings it to her lips. She downs two pills, even though she's only supposed to take one at a time. She's also supposed to take them on a full stomach, but she hasn't eaten since breakfast. She's also only supposed to take three a day, but the two she just swallowed dry are already numbers four and five.

She leans against the building and waits for the pills to take effect. When they do, she'll be able to face them all again.

Ashley closes her eyes and waits.

When Mark finally wakes up, he can't believe it. He's back home in his old room. It's exactly as he had left it. For a few minutes, all he can do is wonder if he's somehow gone back in time.

He sees a row of encyclopedias he doesn't remember ever opening sitting on a bookshelf sandwiched between a set of *Encyclopedia Brown* books and a dozen *Hardy Boys* novels with blue spines. Beside the bookshelf, a stereo sits on a walnut stand—a space framed by speakers filled with vinyl LPs. Mark squints but can't read any of the bands' names or album titles from across the room.

Mark crawls out of bed and puts back on the jeans he was wearing yesterday. He walks across the room and opens the drawers of his dresser. He finds musty-smelling underwear, T-shirts, and socks. He then looks through an old storage trunk and finds yearbooks, cassette tapes, Polaroids of people he doesn't recognize. Amid a pile of old papers, he finds a card from Laura from their first anniversary. He remembers she gave it to him on a night she'd cooked a romantic dinner. He opens it slowly and instantly recognizes her delicate handwriting: *Happy Anniversary. I will always love you.*

Mark shoves the card to the bottom of the trunk.

He moves over to an old corner desk that belonged to his late uncle. While rummaging through papers in one of its drawers he finds a photo of Bottlecap. Mark, Steve, and Gary are playing what must have been their first or second show. They're at the Scene, the only place they played for the first year or so while the band was together. He can't believe how thin he used to be, or how happy he looks in the picture. If there was a mirror in the room, he's sure he wouldn't look that happy now.

On top of the desk is a tattered and bulging manila folder with a yellow Post-it note that reads: *Thought you might like to see this.* It's in his father's handwriting. Mark opens the folder and finds dozens of faded clippings from magazines and newspapers about Bottlecap—reviews of their records, reports of their shows. There's even an article from the *Kitty Courier* about when they first got signed and another about Mark leaving the band: KITTY LOCAL SAYS 'NO' TO FAME.

*Why did he keep all this?*

There's even an article from the *New York Times* about indie bands getting signed by major labels. It was probably the biggest exposure they ever received. Towards the end of the story, there's a quote from Mark: "I don't really care who puts out my record, as long as they get it out there. I just want my music to reach as many people as possible." He doesn't remember the interview, or if he actually said that, but he must have. He flips through a few more clippings and discovers that the stories stop after a certain point. The last one is dated 2004, when Bottlecap was featured in a *Rolling Stone* article entitled "One-hit Wonders from Alternative Nation." He closes the folder and leaves the room.

From the landing outside his door, he smells bacon. He also hears his mom singing to herself above the sound of sizzling. He grins and heads for the kitchen.

Mark walks down the stairs, passing row after row of pictures of himself. He watches himself vary in age with each step. At one step he's just a baby; at another is the glossy senior portrait he hadn't wanted to take. All the photos range from his birth to his teenage years. At the bottom, he glances around for more photos, for some picture that wasn't taken when he was a kid, but there are none. There are only more pictures of him as a baby, as a first-grade student, as a third-grade student.

"Hello, Mr. Sleepyhead." His mom is standing in the hallway, wearing a pink and yellow housecoat over blue pajamas. She has a fork in one hand and tongs in the other. "It's about time you woke up."

He leans in for a hug. Mark can't believe how small she feels in his arms. He knows she'll be gone one of these days, but he didn't expect her to disappear bit by bit.

"Sorry I was so late last night. I hope I didn't wake you."

She pulls back and smiles at him. Smiling, she resembles the young woman holding him in all those photos.

"You didn't wake me, son. If I can sleep through your father's snoring, I can sleep through anything."

Mark follows her into the kitchen. She flips over a few pieces of bacon and then pulls a carton of juice from the refrigerator. Mark sees slices of white bread sitting next to a large bowl filled with beaten eggs. He helps himself to coffee.

"Where's dad?"

"Went downtown to get his hair cut."

Mark grins.

"Wants to look good for my big concert next week?"

She turns to him again and, grinning, nods toward the kitchen table.

"He wants to brag."

Mark strolls over and notices a copy of the local newspaper, open to the Arts section, on the Formica tabletop with chrome legs. He sees his own face, staring out in black and white. It's the story he saw online last night.

"Jesus, it's in the actual paper?" He picks it up, quickly scanning it again. "What's dad going to tell them that's not in the story?"

"Oh, it's not so much about that, Mark. He's *proud* of you." She goes to the fridge, returns with maple syrup. "Went down to the Food Lion this morning and must have bought every copy."

Mark laughs and notices that on the fridge there are a bunch of drawings and pieces of paper covered with painted handprints and squiggles.

"My god," he says, pointing. "Have you been hanging on to those for forty years?"

His mom laughs.

"*You* didn't do those, sweetheart. They're new."

"Who did them?"

She shrugs and then puts two slices of bread into the bowl of beaten eggs. She uses a fork to dip them on both sides and then puts them into a frying pan.

"You don't know them." She turns the French toast over, the top sides now brown and golden. "Grandkids of friends of your father."

Mark is aware that all of their friends have grandkids. They go to the weddings of their friends' children, they go to christenings. During their weekly phone calls, his parents tell him the children's names whenever a new one is born—Ruby, Jacob, Theo, Stella. Mark feels bad for letting his parents down, for making them different from everyone they know, for closing them off from that part of life. But he doesn't know what else to do. He's had a few relationships while he's lived in New York, but nothing serious.

His mom puts the French toast on a Melamine plate, along with two pieces of bacon. She places the plate on the table and then returns to the stove. She puts more slices of bread into the frying pan.

Mark sits at the table and digs into the meal. As he's chewing, his phone buzzes. He pulls it out and glances at the glowing screen. It's a text from Gary, his old band mate.

*Dude, did you see the story the paper published about the show?! Call me or Steve as soon as you get this.*

Mark hasn't seen Gary or Steve in twenty years. Not since he left the band by walking out on the recording sessions of their major label debut in Los Angeles back in ninety-three. In the weeks that followed, Mark talked with the confused producer, his pissed off A&R guy, a bunch of clueless executives at the label and, finally, a couple of very friendly and expensive lawyers who sorted the whole thing out. But he never spoke to Gary or Steve. He still hasn't spoken to them in the run up to the reunion show next week. They've traded emails, a few texts, but that's it. Most of his communication has been with Dave, the owner of the label Bottlecap first recorded for. He was given Gary's and Steve's numbers by Dave last month, but has so far never used them.

Mark's not really up for seeing Gary yet. He knows there's going to be some sort of scene when he does, and he wants to put that off for as long as possible. Instead of responding, he texts Dave, asking for his address and setting up a time to meet tomorrow.

Joining Mark at the table with a plate of French toast, his mom nods towards the phone.

"Anything important?"

"Nothing that can't wait."

She cuts her French toast into squares, covers the squares in syrup but, before taking a bite, she speaks.

"It's nice to have you home, Mark."

"Thanks, Mom. It's nice to be home."

Randy is on a break. He's standing in the alley near the employees' entrance where the huge delivery trucks unload their stock. Right now it's empty, except for Randy. He clocked out two cigarettes ago and figures he can fit in another. He fishes one out of the crumpled pack and lights it. The first puff tastes good, but after that he can't taste anything. From the second puff on, it's just a habit. As he takes a drag he sees yellowed fingers and burn marks from when he drunkenly reached for the lit end years ago. His BlackBerry buzzes. He pulls it out of his pocket. It's a text from a number he doesn't recognize.

*Hey loverboy this is Charlene.*

The name doesn't ring a bell.

*It's been weeks. I miss you. Want to get together?*

Randy grins but doesn't respond to the text. As he's putting the phone back in his pocket, Hector comes into the alley. Hector's working the same shift as Randy. Bill assigned him to handle restocking while Randy was on a break. Restocking is just about all that Bill lets Randy do any more. Bill used to let Randy cover the cash register but, whenever he did, the drawer would always come out short.

Randy has worked at Bookstorage for four years. Despite his tenure, his job title's still "associate" and he's barely making more than minimum wage. It's pretty much the same amount he's earned ever since dropping out of college. The jobs change—he's had at least a dozen in the past twenty years—but the pay stays the same.

Hector and Randy nod hello to each other. Hector's young, barely in his twenties. Randy doesn't like him because he has that cocky attitude that comes with being young. Hector also reminds him of Cody and Hunter. Randy hates that being at work feels like being at home.

Hector tosses a half-dozen empty boxes into an industrial-sized Dumpster. Randy recognizes the boxes; he was planning on spending the rest of his shift unpacking those boxes. Hector did it in ten minutes.

*That smug fucking bastard. One day he'll be my age and then he'll realize what a prick he is.*

Hector grins as he re-enters Bookstorage. Randy flicks the half-finished cigarette towards the parking lot and enters the store. He clocks back in and fishes the black Bookstorage vest out of his half-open locker in the employee break room. He always makes sure to take the vest off for his breaks, afraid that someone will walk down the alley and realize he works in a shitty bookstore flanked on one side by a chain pet supplies store and a Christian arts and crafts store on the other.

As Randy puts on the vest, he smells the strong odor of stale cigarette smoke. He walks onto the floor and spots Hector in the new nonfiction section. Hector smirks and points to his watch.

Bill is manning the cash register. He spots Randy and says, "I was about to send out a search party."

Randy doesn't respond. He just stares at the ground, noticing and kicking at the patterns in the carpet.

"Why don't you be in charge of the information desk for the rest of the day," Bill says. "Think you can handle that?"

Randy nods and heads toward the back of the store where a sign reads ASK ME TO HELP YOU FIND YOUR NEXT GREAT READ TODAY. He stands behind a computer terminal that's used primarily to look up stock. From his post he can see Bill, still behind the cash register at the front of the store. Hector's jet-black hair bobs up and down as he unpacks the new releases. That would have taken Randy a week, but Hector will probably be done by closing.

The phone behind the counter rings and, even from the back of the store, Randy hears Bill answer it. While Bill's talking to the customer, Randy quickly logs into the computer built into the information desk. He switches from the Bookstorage stock program to a browser. He checks his email.

He rereads Charles's email from earlier.

*Randy,*

*Hey! This is Charles. Chipp, remember? ;-)*

*Check out the link below. Remember these bands?! Let me know if you want to go. If not, and you just want to get together some time and hang out, that's cool too. It's been too long, dude. Get back to me when you can.*

*Charles*

Randy makes sure Bill is still busy behind the cash register and then clicks on the link. He leans in and scans the story. Randy can't believe it—the Deer Park, Bottlecap, the Disappointed—bands he hasn't thought of in ages. He has records by all of them. At least he used to—they're in storage at his parents' house in Maryland. Randy even has a vague memory of interviewing one of the bands a long time ago for the zine he made back when he lived with Charles. They'd gone to college together but were friends from even before that, ever since meeting in high school. They were inseparable for the subsequent six years.

After they stopped being roommates, Charles started taking classes at night in order to complete his degree. Charles offered to send Randy all the info so that he could go back to school, too, but Randy never took him up on it. Last he heard, Charles was married, had a kid, and was living in Tiger Bay.

Randy goes back to his email. He writes a quick response to Charles, saying *Sure, seeing the concert sounds cool.* Just as he's sending the email, Bill walks by on the way to his office. As he passes, Randy clicks back to the Bookstorage system, trying to look alert. It's not convincing. Bill just shakes his head.

Charles can't find the conference room. The fifteenth floor is just one long anonymous stretch of cubicles, micro-kitchens, photocopiers, reams of paper stacked up like bricks, mail cubbies, closed office doors, and the occasional conference room, none of which is the one he's looking for. He glances at his watch, a silver Breitling that cost four grand. He bought it as a present to himself when he became Senior Director two years ago. It's the thing to do when you get a promotion. This means that, at a big company like Trust Insurance, everyone at Charles's level and above has a nice watch. At lunch, they compare them and pass them around.

*11:57. I'm almost late.*

He rounds another corner and looks for someone from whom he can ask directions, but all he sees is row after row of empty cubicles. Everyone's already left for lunch.

*I hate the fifteenth floor.*

Charles storms down a hallway that looks the same as every other hallway in the building. He rounds yet another corner and passes a conference room—a smaller one, not the one he's looking for—which he's positive he's passed before. Now he's convinced he's going in circles. The Breitling seems to burn on his arm. He glances down. 12:07.

Up ahead, he spots Jack from sales and Trina from PR getting off the elevator. They're attending the same meeting he is, so Charles speeds up and falls into step behind them. Charles can tell they're chatting about the new tenth-floor receptionist whom nobody likes. He joins the conversation.

"And always with the attitude," Charles says. "Am I right?"

Trina turns and says, "Charles, where did you swoop in from?"

"Oh, you know, the usual."

"Yeah, well, I'm glad we found you," Jack says. "I can never find this goddamn conference room." Charles notices that there's sweat running along Jack's upper lip.

Finally they come to what looks like a dead end made up of row after row of shoulder-high filing cabinets framed on either side by tall potted plants. He watches as Trina disappears behind what must be a gap between the plants and the filing cabinets. Jack follows Trina, seeming to vanish into thin air. Charles had passed this way at least three times in the past fifteen minutes, but always kept walking.

On the other side, at the far end of a long hallway, is a door through which Charles can see Dylan, Brooks, and a few others from the twelfth floor. Jack, Trina, and Charles enter the conference room. Trina immediately gravitates towards Tanya and Bonnie, two more women in PR. Jack, unable to find anyone from the sales department, sticks close to Charles.

Charles is relieved to see that the meeting hasn't started. Everyone's just standing around exchanging pleasantries, gossip, and talking about how they spent their weekend. Charles walks over to where Dylan and Brooks are standing by a window that overlooks downtown Kitty.

"Charles, looking good this morning," Brooks says. "I like the tie."

Charles grabs the tip—red silk with purple and orange paisley—and looks at it as if he's never seen it before.

"What," he says, "this old thing?"

Dylan leans in, punches him on the shoulder.

"Don't bullshit a bullshitter. I think you deserve that promotion. Not more than I deserve it, of course."

Charles just grins and punches him back before he takes a seat. Brooks and Dylan sit down, too, on either side of Charles. Jack—who had been loitering at the edge of the trio—suddenly looks put out, like they're playing musical chairs and there isn't a place for him to sit. He meekly moves across the room and is forced to take a seat with his back to the screen.

"Loved the report you wrote, Charles, about the west coast sales projections," Brooks says. "I think they're inflated, too. I bet you get a trip to headquarters out of that."

Charles thinks that Brooks is being genuine but, around the office, you never can tell. Some people are out for your job; and if you don't figure that out in time, they'll get it. Brooks has only been at Trust for six months and doesn't quite know his way around. Charles figures that's why he's cozying up to him, learning where the fault lines are, finding out who's important and who's not.

*Brooks is a smart kid. I should ask him to lunch.*

Someone Charles doesn't know—he looks slightly familiar, but Charles doesn't remember who he is or where in the company he works—gets his attention from across the table and says, "I just sent you an email."

"Great," Charles says, "great!" He then turns to face Dylan, pretending to ask him something but can't because he's playing Angry Birds on his iPhone. So Charles decides to check his email instead.

He has three new emails from people he doesn't know. He wonders if any of them are from the guy across the table. All three emails are bullshit, and Charles deletes them without responding. He checks Gmail and sees that Randy has written back. Charles writes a quick response, telling Randy to get a ticket to the concert while pledging to do the same. Charles looks up and sees Sharon—a junior employee on Dylan's team—enter the conference room. She slips Dylan a file folder and then takes the last seat at the table. Charles thinks it's odd that Sharon, who's not even a manager, was invited to the meeting.

*Keep an eye on Sharon. And Dylan. They're up to something.*

"Gentlemen," O'Brien says (even though there are women present), "let's begin."

The lights are turned down and the blinds are drawn. The room takes on the red glow of the Trust logo: a red fireman's shield resembling a coat of arms containing the icons of a car, a house, and the silhouettes of a nuclear family—man, woman, little boy and girl.

O'Brien starts by discussing Trust's share price and current place in the market. He then highlights a few ads for the upcoming fall marketing campaign before going into Trust's Q2 results and this branch's Q3 goals. After about ten minutes it seems like O'Brien's getting through his slides at a good pace, and no one's asking any questions, so Charles is hopeful the meeting will last less than the scheduled ninety minutes.

Charles's phone buzzes in his pocket. A text.

He feels self-conscious at first—checking his phone while O'Brien's in the middle of what's supposed to be an important presentation—but Charles can see that a number of others are doing the same thing, staring at their phones or else typing away on laptops. This happens all the time during meetings. No one ever pays attention. They treat whoever's speaking like a TV; looking at their phone is their way of changing the channel. The strangest thing is that nobody seems to mind, not even O'Brien. Charles is even sure that at one point—during the middle of his own presentation—O'Brien himself glances down at his phone.

The text is from Grace.

*The contractor we liked just confirmed he can start on the roof by June. But we need to book him right now or we may lose him to another job. And he's going to need half up front.*

Ten thousand dollars. Charles can pull that much together if he empties his savings account, but after that he'd have nothing else. He's not due for a bonus until next year and a raise—since he was promoted just last fall—would be even farther off.

He writes back.

*Tell him I need more time to decide.*

Grace responds instantly.

*Darling, we may lose him. And we need to get it fixed. For Maddie. Please.*

Charles begins to nervously drum his fingers on the table. First Dylan notices, and then Brooks, so he stops. He writes back to Grace.

*A week. Tell him to give me a week.*

Seconds later, the reply.

*OK.*

Charles is about to put his iPhone back into his pocket when it buzzes yet again. This time it's an email from Tom, Trust's southern district manager and O'Brien's right-hand man. There's no subject header, a power move that says *I'm too fucking busy to tell you what this email is about.* Charles opens the email. The message reads: *If you have some time this week, I'd love to talk.*

Charles looks across the table and can see Tom staring at his iPhone, sitting to O'Brien's right. Charles writes back.

Of course. I'd love to. I'll set up some time with Heather.

Charles watches as Tom reacts to the buzzing of his phone, Charles's email having been beamed up to space before hurtling back down to earth seconds later. In the semi-darkness, Charles can register Tom giving him a quick nod.

Charles's heart begins to race. He thinks of the vice president rumor, and how much he needs that job. Sweat begins to break out on his forehead. He's in a daze as he hears O'Brien end his presentation by saying, "And so, let's have another great quarter."

When the lights come on, everyone claps except Charles.

Craig is Googling Ashley. He finally finds her on LinkedIn. He can't believe it, but she still lives in the area. She works for some sort of non-profit environmental company just outside of town. He looks over her résumé. Fourth down on the list is where she worked when they dated. He imagines her getting ready for each of the interviews that led to these new jobs. She must have been excited. She must have done research. She must have debated, the night before, about what to wear and then celebrated after the interviews went well and then again when she got the job. He hadn't been part of any of it.

There's even a photo of her—a thumbnail to the left of her name—near the top of the page. Craig's about to click on it when he's distracted by two guys in his office wearing kilts who begin to juggle huge things that look like bowling pins. He tries to ignore them, but the rhythmic back and forth, back and forth of the clubs begins to put him in a trance.

Craig doesn't have an office, just a desk—a cheap plank of Ikea particleboard with four steel legs. No filing cabinet, no bookshelves, no walls. No pictures, no personal mementos. Nothing but a monitor and some cables for plugging in the laptop he carries with him from meeting to meeting. The only thing that distinguishes Craig's desk from the three others shoved up against it, which form one of three quartets of desks placed around the loft-like room, are his gray headphones. All the office employees wear headphones when they sit at their desks. The coders wear them to "stay in the zone," heads down as they focus only on huge Thunderbolt monitors while they blast trance music. On the desk next to his sit a pair of red head-phones. On the desk across from Craig's sits a half-empty bowl of dry Frosted Flakes, along with a pair of huge black headphones with white skulls over the ears.

One of the coders, sitting on the opposite side of the room from the jugglers, takes off his headphones and tosses them onto his desk. As the coder walks toward the mini-kitchen in the middle of the room, Craig can hear the *thump thump thump* of the bass seep out of the headphones and, for a few seconds, the jugglers are in perfect time with the beat. The coder reaches into the fridge, grabs a beer, and pries off the cap with a bottle opener on a chain that's attached to his jeans. He tosses the cap into a trashcan stuffed with empty beer bottles and half-filled take-out food containers. The cap bounces off a Slurpee cup and lands on the floor where it joins five others, making a big-dipper shape on the discolored carpet. Seatr reminds Craig of college, except more gets done at college.

Craig turns back to his laptop and clicks on the photo of Ashley. It gets bigger, taking up almost half the screen. He loses his breath for a moment. Craig occasionally has thought about Ashley over the years, but he's never seen a recent picture of her. All of the photos he has of her, or the two of them together, are inside a suitcase in the storage locker at his condo.

The first thing he notices is her hair; it's considerably shorter than it was when they lived together. Her hair used to fall past her shoul-ders and was all one length, but now she has bangs and the sides barely cover her ears. The color is different, too—darker than he remembers. She used to be almost blonde, but now her hair is light brown. Craig can't remember if she was coloring it back then or if what he's seeing now comes from a bottle, masking gray. Her eyes also look different—more sunken—or maybe she was tired when the photo was taken. Or maybe it's just that she's older.

He stares at the screen, finding it hard to believe he has any con-nection to the person in the picture, or that they'd ever laughed or cried or slept together. It's just a picture of a person. It could be any-one. It could be a stranger. He has to force himself to remember Ash-ley's voice or the two of them together in any capacity. He even tries to remember her naked, but can't recall any details beyond the generic curves and body parts every woman has.

Below Ashley's picture there's an envelope icon and the words SEND ASHLEY EMAIL. He clicks on the envelope and a pop-up window appears with fields for a subject header and message. He quickly fills in the boxes—typing quickly so that he doesn't lose his nerve or give any thought to what he's about to do after all this time. He hits the blue SEND button. The window disappears and is replaced with a box that says THANK YOU YOUR EMAIL HAS BEEN SENT.

He exhales and then looks up, his breath now shallow and quick. He spots Josh entering the office, back from his lunch with the board. Craig's dismayed to see Josh walk right up to his desk.

"Hey, can we chat a minute?"

Craig closes his laptop and says, "Sure."

The desk next to Craig's has an orange inflatable yoga ball instead of a chair. Josh rolls it over and sits on it.

"I just want to make sure you're comfortable with all the feedback we gave you earlier."

"What, in the board meeting? Yeah, sure, I get it." He sinks into his chair, trying to appear casual. "It's all good."

"I know it means basically starting over from what your strategy had been initially." Josh bounces up and down on the yoga ball as he speaks, his eyes becoming a moving target for Craig to follow. "But I think you'll see that it's better this way."

Craig nods, but doesn't add anything. Seconds go by. In the corner, the jugglers are still juggling and, even though the coder has returned to his desk and put his headphones back on, Craig can still hear the bass.

"So you grok what I'm saying?"

"Grok?" Half the time Craig's not sure what Josh is talking about. He speaks literally in code, using bits of computer jargon or nerd slang that everyone at Seatr except Craig seems to know. "Totally, I . . . yes—*grokked*. One hundred percent."

"Good," Josh says, still bouncing. "Basically, you're thinking linear. I need you to think horizontal."

More bouncing. More juggling. More *thump thump thump*.

"Horizontal, yup. *Totally* get it."

"I'm glad."

Craig's now bobbing in his chair while trying to follow Josh's eyes as they rise and fall, rise and fall.

"It's just I was saying that if we keep pushing to get users before the product's fully functioning, it might—"

"Craig, Craig, Craig." Josh is waving his hands back and forth. "You're forgetting. We're in beta."

"I know that, Josh, but we're also live. The site's up and running. We're getting traffic and people are trying to buy—"

Josh cuts him off by saying, "Beta, Craig. *Bay-tuh.*"

He gets up, sending the yoga ball rolling across the room where it runs into an X-box Rock Band set up. The collision sends plastic guitars and drums crashing to the floor. Josh doesn't react. Instead, he crosses the office, heading for the conference room. As he walks, Josh is repeating, "Beta. Beta." The jugglers don't pause to let Josh by. Instead, Josh times his walk so that he perfectly knits himself inside the pattern of the dancing pins. One second he's in front of them, the next second he's behind.

Josh enters the conference room and slams the door. Seconds later, the word "Beta!" ricochets throughout the office.

Ashley parks her Prius in the driveway, pulling up alongside Andrew's old red Audi with faded Greenpeace and Obama bumper stickers. Neither of them parks in the garage because it's filled with junk— cardboard boxes full of clothes they swore they'd donate, nearly empty paint cans she has no idea why they're keeping, gardening equipment they never use for the garden they never planted. This would embarrass Ashley except almost all of her neighbors do it as well. Pretty much everyone up and down Euclid Street parks their cars in their driveways, every garage being too packed with stuff. There's even a single guy at the end of the block who keeps two motorcycles in his driveway, so he parks a Dodge Charger on his lawn. There's a patch of yellowed grass and near-dirt where the car always sits. There is only one house on the street whose owners use their garage for their cars— a young couple who moved in last summer, always seen walking at dusk and holding hands. Ashley hates them.

On the front step, she discovers a large cardboard box. Ashley bends over to pick it up, bracing herself for the weight a box of this size must contain. She's surprised when the box is almost weightless. It feels empty. She looks at the return address. Local. It's addressed to Andrew. She enters the house.

"Honey, I'm home." But she says it in a whisper.

Ashley kicks off her heels, closes and locks the door behind her. On a table in the entryway there's a huge stack of junk mail, bills, and magazines. She places her bag on the teetering pile.

"Andrew?"

*What day is this? Maybe it's a day he's teaching. I need to get one of those apps for my phone. Something to keep track of my appointments. And Andrew.*

She walks through the house, carrying the box and looking for her husband. She finds him in his office off the kitchen, sitting at a desk, surrounded by books. In the middle of the desk is a laptop, the glowing screen the only light in the room until Ashley flips a switch just inside the entrance. He has bare feet and is wearing sweatpants and a T-shirt inside out. His thinning hair is scattered in all directions.

"You'll hurt your eyes."

"Thanks."

"You eat yet?"

"An hour ago." Andrew's still staring at the screen of his laptop. "Leftover pasta from last night. You?" Ashley squints and can see sentences and paragraphs.

"We ordered at the office." She holds up the box. "What's this?"

Andrew looks up, registering her presence for the first time. His eyes, difficult to distinguish behind his thick-framed glasses, glance at the box and stay fixed on it.

"Good, it arrived."

Ashley looks at the label.

"What's Pill W?"

"It's pronounced *pillow.*"

Ashley protests, "But it's spelled P-I-L-L-W."

"It's a website."

He turns back to his computer. She drops the box on the floor.

"I love how these websites feel they can just randomly misspell words," Ashley says. "It's not like letters are expensive."

Andrew stops typing and grabs a copy of a Richard Yates novel. As he flips through it, Ashley can see blocks of highlighted text and Andrew's chicken scratch in the margins. She says, "So, what's in the box?"

"A pillow. It's from a new subscription service, based here in Kitty. They send you a new pillow every month."

"What for?"

"For variety." After a few seconds, he adds, "They're disrupting sleep."

"Why?"

"What do you mean?"

"Sleep. You don't *want* to disrupt sleep, right? Isn't that the whole point?"

Andrew sighs.

"As an industry," he says. "I mean, as a *business*. Everything's got to be disrupted sooner or later. Netflix did it with video; iTunes did it with music."

"And now Pillw's doing it . . . for sleep."

"Someone had to."

"How much does it cost?"

"Fifty dollars a month."

Ashley pokes at the hardwood floor with her left foot, noticing that the toe of her black stocking has a hole in it.

"Do you send the pillows back?"

"Of course not. Don't be silly."

She pulls a chair from the kitchen table and sets it in the doorway to Andrew's office. She sits down. "How's the novel coming?"

"Good, good. I Skyped with Tina—"

"Tina?"

"Tina from my writing group. I Skyped with Tina this morning and she thinks I'm on the right track. Now it's just a matter of finishing it."

Andrew has always wanted to be a writer. After failing to get anything published in his twenties, he went back to school to get his teaching degree. But in the past couple of years, he's started again. Essays and articles. Book reviews. His stuff appears on a few websites. He doesn't get paid, but he doesn't seem to mind. And now he's working on a novel. It keeps him happy. It keeps him busy. It keeps him away from her.

"Andrew?" Ashley says.

Still typing. Not looking up. "Yes?"

"Do you ever think about children? For us. About us having children, I mean."

When Andrew stops typing, there's nothing but silence. It's something she never liked about this neighborhood. It's *too* quiet.

"Is it time again for *that* talk?"

She doesn't respond.

"We agreed," Andrew says. "We agreed a long time ago. And now it's too late. You're forty-three, almost forty-four. The chances are . . ."

"It'd be a chance." She begins to tear up, her throat tight.

Andrew just looks away. Normally the talk doesn't go this far. As of late it's been less of a discussion and more of a bullet point, a statement of fact. How do you argue with time? With age? You don't.

"I'm sorry," she says.

"No, I'm sorry."

She fights the urge to repeat, *No, I'm sorry*. Instead, she says, "I'm going upstairs to do some work."

She begins to walk down the hallway, first to pick up her bag and then to head upstairs. Andrew calls out.

"Your doctor called."

Startled, Ashley stops. She backtracks a bit, walking on tiptoe. She doesn't know why.

"What?"

"Your doctor," he says. "I guess you called him yesterday about getting another refill on your prescription for Pixilate or Potreronon or whatever that stuff is called."

"Protraxanon. Yeah, so?"

"So, he's going to need you to come in for another appointment before he gives you a refill. You're going through that stuff too fast. He says, and I quote, 'You are exceeding the recommended dosage.'"

Ashley runs her tongue against her teeth. They feel scratchy. She wonders if that's a side effect, or if she just needs to go to the dentist.

"So, are you going to go see him again?"

Her face goes flush. She thinks of Craig's email from earlier in the day. She's still not sure if she's going to respond.

*After all this time, what could he want?*

"See who?"

"Your doctor. I thought you saw him just a week ago."

"Oh," Ashley says. "*Him.*"

Andrew laughs.

"Who did you think I meant?"

"No one. And no, I'm *not* going to see him again." She looks down the hallway, toward the stairs. "It was bad enough last time. All his stupid questions."

"Ashley, he *needs* to ask all those questions. After all, maybe that's the wrong stuff for you. Maybe you need something else. Or nothing at all."

"I don't like doctors."

"I know."

"I don't need some doctor knowing all about . . . no one needs to know . . . anything."

"Not even me?"

"No, Andrew." She starts walking away. "Not even you."

Mark is driving through town. He couldn't sleep. Being in his old room was freaking him out, so now he's guiding his rental car through a nearly deserted Kitty. It's not even late, just a bit after eleven, but everything's closed, even the bars. Only gas stations seem to be open.

The town looks more or less the way he remembers it. Before he came back to Kitty he tried to imagine what it'd be like, how the town might have changed over the last twenty years. He guessed it would be built up, more crowded than it used to be, a bigger city than he remembered. Stoplights where there used to be just stop signs. Houses where there used to be vacant lots. Chain restaurants as far as the eye could see. But it's almost the opposite. At dinner his dad told him about some new area in town that's been recently renovated—a number of old warehouses housing a bunch of new tech companies—but

Mark doesn't see any evidence of that growth here. He keeps passing strip malls with empty stores, dilapidated churches, and cheap-looking restaurants with signs out front. LUNCH SPECIAL $4.95 MONDAY–THURSDAY, ALL-DAY SPECIALS $5.95.

While stuck at a red light, Mark notices that the Food Lion—the grocery store he used to go to all the time—is still there. The façade has been redone in red brick and white trim, which makes the whole building look more grand and colonial. Back when Mark used to go here it was a sort of mustard yellow. Further along the parking lot, where there used to be a record store, there's now an Office Depot. Anchoring the parking lot at each end are fast food restaurants that weren't there before, a Chick-fil-A at one end and a Waffle House at the other.

Further down the street he notices a huge Starbucks where there used to be a small Italian restaurant he and Laura would go to whenever either of them had cash, which wasn't often. The BP gas station is gone, replaced by a new one with the same green and yellow colors, only now it's called El Cheapo and has a banner across the front that reads DISCOUNT CIGARETTES. Mark pulls over and parks. There are parking meters everywhere, which hadn't been the case when he was growing up.

Turning the corner, he sees Heck Music on the far corner sandwiched between a tanning salon and another gas station. This is where Mark's parents bought his first guitar and where he later took lessons from an ex-hippie in an upstairs room filled with boxes of sheet music.

He walks up the street to where the Scene used to be. Mark already knows it's out of business. The first question he asked Dave when he was contacted about the reunion show was whether or not it'd be at the Scene. Mark thought it'd be fitting since that's where Bottlecap played their first and last shows. But Dave told him it had closed years ago. Besides, the reunion was a benefit and they needed to raise some cash. Even after Bottlecap had gained a local following and could easily sell out the small club, they never earned more than a grand playing there.

Halfway up the block, he sees the new sign which reads JAKE'S BAR AND GRILL. Underneath this it says TAP BEER. Where kids used to line up to see bands, there's now an outdoor patio with chairs and tables. Mark approaches the front window and leans against the glass, cupping his hands around his eyes to see inside. He sees two pool tables and an ATM machine. Lit neon signs for Coors Light and Budweiser hang above the bar where the last employee is washing mugs for the next day. In the far corner, he sees four booths packed into where the stage used to be.

*They turned my youth into a sports bar.*

Mark walks back to his rental car. As he leaves the downtown area, the road quickly turns residential. Looking from side to side, Mark recognizes certain houses from when he lived in the area—the modern one he was always curious about, the one on stilts so it'd have a view of downtown, the mansion he never envied. After a few turns, he sees it. The fourplex apartment, the last place he lived in Kitty before moving away: 121 South Euclid. He parks the rental car where he used to park his own car all of those years ago.

It looks exactly the same: red brick with white windows and black shutters; two white columns supporting a shingled awning with a black door and a black mailbox; two stories, four apartments; two upstairs, two downstairs. His was the one on the bottom right. The only thing he doesn't recognize is a wooden enclosure on the corner of the lawn for three trashcans and two blue recycling bins.

The blinds are down, but he remembers the layout. The large window in the front, to the right of the door, was the living room. The smaller window next to this was the front bedroom. That's where he kept his guitar and amp, along with a desk and an old office chair he'd found downtown and rolled all the way home.

All of Bottlecap's songs were written in that room. It's also where he designed all of their early records, fliers, and T-shirts. He later used those skills—after the songwriting royalties from the first big Bottlecap record dried up—to go to New York and get a job designing book covers for Rodney & Co., a publisher in downtown Manhattan. He's now worked there for almost twelve years. He's lived in his rent-controlled studio apartment on the Upper West Side for nearly ten.

The last time he was here was before the band left for Los Angeles. They'd just returned from a short tour and, in just a few days (not that they knew it then), they'd be leaving for LA. Just a month after that, he'd be walking out on the band, on his friends, and the chance of a lifetime. That whole sequence of events was put into motion in the apartment he's staring at.

That period now seems so fraught with significance and yet, at the time, it was just another day. The record deal had come to him so easily he thought it'd be just as easy to get another. They were young— early twenties—and had only been a band for a few years. It was just a hobby. No one expected much from it, so when it turned into something more, no one knew how to act. Mark wished that those days had had a sign on them saying DON'T FUCK THIS UP. THIS IS IMPORTANT. But they didn't. And because of that, that time in his life— when it was happening—looked like any other and he didn't have the wisdom to treat it any differently. There are days you waste and days you savor, but when you're in the moment, you just don't have the wisdom or perspective to tell the two apart.

The headlights of a car coming around the corner flash in his eyes. For a few seconds, all he sees is yellow. But then the scene returns. His old apartment. His home town. He's back.

It begins.

# 2: MY FORGOTTEN FAVORITE

It's ten in the morning and Randy's in his room trying to buy a ticket for the Bottlecap show. He types DARK STAR LOUNGE into the Google search bar on his beat-up MacBook, misspelling *lounge* twice. When the results come back, he has to squint to see. Randy knows he needs glasses, but he's too cheap to buy them. Glasses would cost a hundred bucks. Squinting's free. Besides, if he had that kind of money to spend on anything, he'd spend it on his teeth. His gums are swollen, it hurts when he chews, and he's had six teeth pulled in the last ten years. If he ever has extra money it's going into his mouth, not his eyes.

He tries to click on the first link, but the trackpad's cracked and there's dirt and grime collected in the corners. It takes Randy three tries. The laptop was cutting edge when he bought it brand-new just two years ago, breaking his bank account in the process. Now it feels heavy and thick as a brick compared to Cody and Hunter's MacBook Airs. When Randy was a kid, computers looked like microwaves and had keys the size of sugar cubes. Now they're nothing but a screen the thickness of a fingernail and keys smaller than Scrabble tiles.

*Everything's getting thinner and faster, while I just get fatter and slower.*

The screen finally loads. He clicks on the calendar and adds one ticket to his cart. Then it asks him for his credit card information.

*Shit.*

Randy doesn't have a credit card. He's applied a dozen times, but his credit's so bad he's always turned down. He even tried once with this sketchy outfit he saw on a billboard, run by a check-cashing company in Puerto Rico, but even they wouldn't give him one. So he uses his debit card. After putting in the digits and hitting PLACE ORDER, he does the math in his head.

He had $82 in his checking account the other day. Since then he's bought a few groceries, gas, cigarettes, and lunch at the food court during his Bookstorage shift. Deduct the cost of the ticket, and he's got about $20 until next payday.

He writes a quick note to Charles. Corporate asshole or not, he used to be a friend and Randy doesn't have a lot of those now.

*Chipp ;-)*
*Just bought my ticket for the Bottlecap show. Make sure you do the same. Hope you're well, motherfucka.*

*R*

Randy then clicks over to Facebook. He sees that Bottlecap's old label is posting photos of them from back in the day, playing at the Scene as well as other clubs around Virginia. Randy looks for himself in the crowds, but can't find his face among the blurs in the front row. A few clicks later he discovers that someone's uploaded the first couple of Bottlecap singles—the ones you can't get anymore—onto YouTube. As the music starts playing—*"I've been talking to Stephen Hawking, and he says it's not in the stars for us"*—all of those years come back to him.

He remembers living with Charles in that apartment downtown. Everything in it was stuff they'd found on the street. The coffee table was two milk crates taped together. Pizza boxes stood in for shades. The fridge was only sporadically filled, usually after they'd cashed paychecks from whatever menial jobs they worked at the time. What they bought back then are things he still buys—Kraft Macaroni & Cheese, Chef Boyardee Ravioli, Top Ramen.

Everything back then revolved around the weekend: what band to see, whose party to go to. Randy found out that as he got older it became reversed—everything was about the week. Monday through Friday people went to work, had meetings, did business. The only thing people his age do on the weekends is have brunch. Randy hates brunch.

The Bottlecap song ends, so he clicks onto another.

*"The people who think I'm shit are starting to outnumber those who don't."*

Randy remembers this one, too. He remembers Bottlecap playing it at shows where he knew half the people in the crowd. When it ends, he can see that the same person's also uploaded songs by the Disappointed and the Deer Park—the other bands who are playing next week. Randy hasn't heard this music in decades. He clicks from video to video, group to group, song to song.

Wanting to share this with someone, he pauses the video and listens for the guys. Even above the music coming out of their laptops, Randy can hear Cody and Hunter typing in the kitchen. He grabs his laptop and opens the door, smarting at the fluorescent light from the kitchen. As Randy approaches, Cody and Hunter don't respond; they just keep on typing.

Randy places his laptop onto the center of the kitchen table. It lands with a thud.

"I want you guys to hear this. This is the kind of music I listened to when I was . . ." He can't quite bring himself to finish the sentence by saying *your age*. "It's a local band. From the nineties."

The first song's barely begun before Cody peers over the top of his laptop and says, "What is that? *YouTube*?" He says the word as if a skunk has just sprayed his face.

"What's wrong with YouTube?"

Hunter says, "Cody hates YouTube."

"What?" Randy pauses the video. "Why?"

"You ever read their terms of service?"

"Of course not. Why would I—"

Hunter cuts off Randy by saying, "Cody prefers Vevo."

"Vevo, what's Vevo? I've never even heard of that."

45

Cody and Hunter laugh.

"Maybe he thinks you mean *Vimeo*," Cody says.

"Will you guys stop? I'm trying to talk to you about a band. Don't you care about music?"

"I like music." Hunter raises his laptop. "Look. Music."

Randy listens. The sound is nothing but electronic chirps and beeps. No lyrics, no guitar, no drums.

"That's not music," Randy says. "That's a CD player malfunctioning."

"CD player." Cody stifles laughter. "Who has CDs anymore?"

Randy wants to say *I do*, but he doesn't since his stereo's been out of commission for six months and he hasn't had the cash to fix or replace it. Instead, he says, "I don't even know what bands you listen to. Who do you like?"

"Spotify," Cody says.

"Pandora," Hunter says.

"Those aren't bands, you guys, those are websites."

Cody lowers the screen of his laptop slightly. He never does that. "These days," he says, "websites *are* bands. Think about it. Four guys get together. Each one has a different talent or skill they bring to the group. They pick a name, come up with a concept, produce a product, and launch in their hometown. If it's a success, they expand to the rest of the world. Everybody loves them and they become rich. They're on the covers of magazines and people wear T-shirts with their logo."

Hunter points to the Napster T-shirt he's wearing.

*Fucking Hunter.*

"And when a site gets too big," Cody continues, "or too commercial, no one likes them anymore."

"Like Yahoo," Hunter says.

"Exactly," Cody says.

"Do you think all this makes you *better* than me?" Randy's close to exhaustion. He should still be sleeping. If he were, he wouldn't be going through this. "*We* stood in line for concert tickets. *You* stand in line for phones."

Cody picks up his iPhone. It's the latest model, top of the line. It looks like a smaller version of the monolith in *2001*.

"Have you *seen* my phone?"

Randy grabs his laptop and storms out of the kitchen, heading back into his room. He slams the door.

Maddie's dentist has the same medicinal smell that Charles has hated for forty-five years. What makes it worse is the slightly sweet smell that underpins the acrid. No matter how hard they try to make their goop taste like bubblegum or blueberry or birthday cake, it's still fluoride. It's still disgusting.

Charles is sitting in the waiting room while Maddie gets her teeth cleaned. Behind the front desk, a receptionist fields calls about appointments and questions about insurance. From the other rooms Charles hears drills, muffled voices, and the white noise of suction.

Even though Charles hates going into the office late—whenever he gets in past ten, he's sure that everyone's looking at him with raised eyebrows—he feels immense pride being out with Maddie. Even for mundane things like this. *Especially* for mundane things like this. Charles figures it's easy to take care of Maddie when he's taking her out for ice cream, or to Disneyworld. Stuff like that may make him a hero in her eyes, but that's not what being a parent is all about. Parenting is the boring stuff—running errands, doctor's appointments. That's when he truly feels like a dad.

In his twenties, Charles fancied himself an artist. He did a bit of writing and was into music. He and Randy even started a magazine. One of his favorite writers back then was F. Scott Fitzgerald. To this day Charles thinks of his short story, "Babylon Revisited," especially that moment at the end where the narrator says that "nothing was much good" besides his daughter. It didn't mean much to Charles at twenty, but when he thinks of those words now—and how he wants to keep Maddie close to him for as long as he can—he shudders. He doesn't want to be one of Fitzgerald's distant, drunk dads. Charles knows he'll never be as good an artist as Fitzgerald, but he has a chance to be a better father.

Maddie comes bounding out of the office.

"Daddy, Daddy, Daddy! No cavities!"

As Charles bends down to scoop her up, her forward momentum

almost knocks him down. She's getting too old to be picked up. This is a tragedy for him. He used to sing her to sleep in the crook of his arm, and now she's almost too big to lift.

"Oh, sweetheart, way to go. I *knew* you could do it."

As he returns her to the ground, she hands him a bag containing a travel-sized container of toothpaste, a mini reel of floss, and a new toothbrush.

"Come on, sweetheart. Let's get you to school."

In the car, Maddie says from the backseat, "They wanted to give me a toy, can you believe that? Like I was some kind of little kid. *As if!*"

"You used to love the toy chest." Charles smiles. "I remember one time Dr. Lawrence let you pick out *two* things. I'd never seen you happier."

Maddie kicks the back of his seat and says "Dad" in a way that connotes he's the biggest idiot on the planet. Then she turns serious. "Daddy?"

"Yes, darling?"

"What if you can't come up with the money?"

Charles digs his fingers into the steering wheel.

"What are you talking about, sweetie?"

Maddie now has her feet on the armrest between the two front seats. Grace never lets Maddie do that, but Charles doesn't mind. She says, "I heard you and Mommy fighting this morning after that man with all the tools on his belt left."

The contractor who's going to fix the roof stopped by to talk scheduling. The schedule looked fine. The problem was money. When the contractor left, Charles and Grace fought in the kitchen about the cost and where they were going to get the cash. They thought Maddie was upstairs.

"Darling, listen to me." Charles speaks slowly and with confidence, trying to also convince himself. "We're going to be okay. We just need to fix the house a bit, and—well, it's going to be expensive."

"But you're going to pay him, right? We're not going to have to live in a broken house, are we?"

At a stoplight he finds her eyes in the rearview mirror and sees fear. This kills him. He has always wanted to protect her, and that look in her eyes means he's failing.

"Madeline, darling, I *promise*."

Charles pulls up to her school. The kids are at recess and Maddie instantly spots a pack of girls to which she belongs. On the way to the office to sign her in, he insists on a kiss goodbye. Maddie begrudgingly delivers one so rapidly Charles doesn't believe it really happened. It hurts his feelings that she's so embarrassed by him.

*Maybe if I were cooler. Maybe if I had hair. Maybe if I were a celebrity.*

He watches as she's greeted by friends. It's all smiles and laughing as they run off, getting lost in the crowd. Charles knows that this process is going to be repeated. He'll lose her first to college, then some strange city, and finally to a husband, a family, her own life. The idea fills him with equal amounts of terror and pride.

By the time he gets to work, it's practically time for lunch. He pulls into the Trust parking lot and begins circling around until he finds a spot. He hustles into the building, hoping he doesn't pass anyone from the sixteenth floor on his way in. Up on twelve, Dylan sees him and grins. He points to his watch, a Rolex.

*Cocksucker.*

Charles passes by Brooks's office and sees him hunched over his keyboard typing away. The keys make a plastic clicking sound. That noise didn't exist twenty-five years ago, yet that's now the soundtrack to the world. He waves as he passes. Brooks waves back.

Charles enters his office and sits down. As he logs into his computer, Jack from Sales walks by and waves. Charles nonchalantly waves back. For all Jack knows, Charles has been here all morning. Charles grins, feeling like he's getting away with something. He checks his email, hoping to see something from Tom or at least from Tom's assistant, Heather, about scheduling the meeting Tom mentioned. But instead there's just a bunch of crap from different departments bugging him about stuff. *Delete, delete, forward to someone else to handle, delete.* He clicks over to Gmail and notices there's a message from his old friend, Randy. It looks like Randy has gotten a ticket to the concert next week. Charles is about to buy a ticket of his own when the office phone rings. He can see from the caller ID it's Tom's assistant. Charles clears his throat and reaches for the phone.

"This is Charles."

"Charles, hi. This is Heather from Tom's office. Tom would like to know if you're free to come by tomorrow at eleven for a chat. Does that work for you?"

Even though this sounds like a question, it's not. When anyone on the sixteenth floor wants to talk to you, you cancel whatever else you're doing.

"That sounds great, Heather, thanks. I'll see you then."

He hangs up the phone. He lets out a breath and then holds his face in his hands.

*I need that job. Goddamnit, I need that job.*

He suddenly hears a knock and looks up. It's Dylan.

"You planning on doing any work today, Charles? Or are you just going to sit around all day?"

Dylan grins and then walks away, cackling.

*Fucking cocksucker.*

Mark pulls up to Dave's house. It's a one-story ranch with peeling paint and a patch of dirt for a front yard. Instead of a garage there's just a carport covering an ancient Volvo, old patio furniture, and some tools. Above the mailbox the big tin letters which spell out the name ROW-LAND are covered in rust.

Mark gets out of the rental car and walks up the front steps. On both sides of the walkway, half-buried in dirt, are supermarket circulars, fliers, and free newspapers still in their plastic bags. The white paint on the door is peeling. When he knocks, his knuckles come back dusty with dirt.

"Holy shit," Dave says, opening the door. "Mark Pellion! Is that you?!"

He's put on about twenty pounds since Mark last saw him. He's now also wearing glasses with cheap-looking brown plastic frames. His sideburns are huge, hanging below each ear like flaps from the hat of his brown curly hair. He's wearing jeans, no shoes, and a blue T-shirt inside out. He pulls Mark in for a hug.

"Good to see you again," Mark says, pulling away.

"Yeah, yeah," Dave says. "Come on in and take a look at the old homestead, such as it is."

Dave steps aside and Mark enters. The house smells like dust, mold, and stale cigarette and pot smoke. There are piles of stuff everywhere. Old magazines, CDs and LPs, bulging manila folders held closed with huge red rubber bands.

Dave says, "Have a seat."

Mark looks around but can't really find a place to sit. Every surface is covered in some kind of junk.

"Sorry." Dave removes a stack of books from a corner of the couch so Mark can sit down. Dave dumps the books onto a stack of posters sitting next to the fireplace. He grabs a barstool from the kitchen and brings it into the living room.

"So, man, how *are* you? How's it feel to be home again?"

"It's okay," Mark says. "A little weird, I guess."

"Yeah, I bet."

Dave leans over and grabs a pack of cigarettes from the top of the TV. He lights one, takes two huge drags, and then ashes into a coffee mug. This reminds Mark of one of his old lyrics: *using a saucer as an ashtray.*

"Well, it's good to see you again, man. It's been too long. Too long."

Mark just nods.

"Looking forward to the show?"

"Yeah, yeah," Mark says. "I guess."

"Cool. Speaking of which, and not to be a dick or anything, but I hear from Gary that you haven't reached out to him yet."

"Oh, yeah. Gary texted me, but I haven't—I didn't text him back. What's up?"

"What's up, Mark, is that he's renting a practice space for you guys to rehearse in. The show's in less than two weeks, you know. It's practically just a week away."

Mark kicks at old copies of the *Kitty Courier* sitting on the floor.

"Yeah, I know. And that's a good idea. Have him send me the address. In the meantime, I've been listening to the old songs. I've been practicing."

"*All* the old songs?"

"What's that supposed to mean?"

"I mean, the songs from the *other* record. The one they finished without you."

"Yes, Dave, even *that* record. I'm an adult, Jesus. The gig's going to be fine. I've done my homework. Don't worry."

"Yeah, but it's not just you. There's Gary and Steve, remember? Don't you think you might need some time?"

"For what?"

"I don't know. Chemistry?"

"We'll be okay, all right? You'll get a nice chunk of change and everything will be fine." Still kicking at the newspapers at his feet, Mark remembers something from the other day. "Speaking of which, I saw the story."

"Wasn't that cool?" Dave polishes his fingernails on his T-shirt. "I drummed that up myself. The editor's an old friend of mine. I used to date his sister. Until he told me not to."

Mark grins. As much as he hates to admit it, he did get a kick out of seeing himself in the paper. His dad's still carrying it around with him wherever he goes.

"And, guess what, man?" Dave says. "I got you another one."

"Another what?"

"Another interview, dude."

"What? With who?"

Dave gets off his barstool and walks to a coffee table covered in scraps of paper. He comes back with a bar napkin.

"Guy named Seth." He offers Mark the napkin. Mark doesn't want to touch it. "He saw the article in the paper and got in touch. Wants to talk to you this week."

Mark turns to the wall. All he sees are stains.

"I don't know, Dave. I haven't done an interview in a long time."

"Come on, Mark. It's for the *Times-Dispatch*, not some rinky-dink little rag from around here. And we're lucky because the guy lives in Kitty. Plus, this one won't just be about Bottlecap. It's a bigger article. It'll cover the other bands, too. The Deer Park guys are all over it. They're meeting with him right now, in fact."

"I don't know, Dave. I don't want too many people to—"

"Too many people to what, Mark? To know about the show? To come see you guys play?"

He doesn't answer, but Dave can tell that's what he meant.

Mark finally says, "It's been twenty years, Dave, since I've played those songs. Since I've been on stage. That's a long time."

"I know, Mark. And I'm not saying you guys are going to be like you used to, but it'll be better than nothing. It'll be better than, you know, not even trying."

Mark shrugs his shoulders. He's not so sure Dave's right. Maybe nothing would have been better. Maybe he should have stayed in New York.

"Look, Mark, just *talk* to the guy, okay?" When he doesn't answer, Dave adds, "The whole world doesn't revolve around you, you know."

"What's that supposed to mean?"

Now Dave shrugs. He says, "There's a lot riding on this. For me. For Gary and Steve. For the guys in the other bands."

On the wall, in the kitchen, Mark sees a poster for one of the first Bottlecap seven inches. He designed it in the apartment he saw last night. He has a copy of it, too, in a storage facility in Chelsea near the Westside Highway. Every year or so, when he goes there to store yet more stuff that doesn't fit into his apartment, he pulls out his old box of Bottlecap stuff. He'll spend ten or twenty minutes fingering the records, flipping through posters, stickers, fliers. He doesn't know what to make of any of it anymore.

"What are you saying, Dave? You still want to be famous? To 'make it'? You're not a kid anymore."

He pokes at his gut and says, "What, you think I don't know that? But who's to say I can't keep making art?"

A stack of old Violent Revolution records sitting on a table catches Mark's eye. On top is a CD compilation from the Disappointed. Perennial also-rans, even in Kitty, the band only ever headlined the Scene during the middle of the week. Never even toured beyond Virginia. Mark wonders what those guys are doing now. He figures that, in about a week, he'll find out.

"You think what we did back in the nineties was *art*?"

Dave snatches the CD out of Mark's hands.

"Well, we certainly weren't wasting our time. Because if we were . . ." Dave stops and looks around the room.

Mark's about to speak when a kid outside on the sidewalk makes noise. At first it's cackling laughter but then, a muffled fall, followed by tears. The sound of a mom comforting the crying child gets fainter and fainter as they sprint home for a Band-Aid and Bactine.

"Look, maybe you don't need this," Dave says. "The money or anything. You're up there in Manhattan, and that's a million miles from here. But I need that cash. It may not seem like a lot to you, but it is to me."

Mark doesn't tell him that one of the reasons he's never come home is because he doesn't want to have to tell anyone how small his life is in New York. He knew people assumed, because it was the Big Apple, that he was living large. He used to stay away because of questions about his past. Why did he do what he did back in the Bottlecap days? Why did he walk out on the band? But, more and more, he stays away from Kitty because of questions about his present and future.

Mark finally says, "I'll do the best I can, Dave. With everything. I promise."

Dave slaps him on the back.

"That's my boy." He glances down at the napkin and squints. "Let's see, for the interview. He'll meet you at the Dark Star Lounge—"

"Where the concert is?"

"Yes, Mark, where the concert is. Thank you for paying attention. He'll meet you there Thursday at five. Okay?"

Mark reaches out and takes the napkin. He can see it's from Jake's Bar and Grill. He says, "Okay."

Ashley's been in meetings all day. Ever since she arrived at work a little after 9:00 AM she's ping-ponged back and forth from meeting to meeting, conference room to conference room, office to office. She calculated once how much time she spent in meetings and, over the course of a year, it added up to a month. Four weeks of her life each year was spent in small rooms with people she doesn't really like. She imagines spending a month in Paris or Rome, or on a beach somewhere doing nothing but drinking cocktails and soaking up the sun. She'd prefer any of that to meetings.

Now that she has a few seconds to spare—there's something on her calendar starting at four o'clock and going until the end of the day, she can't even remember what it is—she goes into her email to look again at Craig's message from yesterday. She reads it over and over, trying to decide if she should write back.

*Ashley,*

*Hi, it's been a long time, I know. I hope you're well and that you don't mind me reaching out to you. And not that I don't think of you often—which of course I do—but I thought of you today when I saw an article (check out the link below) about a bunch of bands getting back together that we used to like. Seeing those names brought back all the years we spent together and, because of that, I had to write.*

*I know that things ended badly between us, but that was a long time ago and I thought, well, I don't know. Just that I would reach out and say hello. I hope you'll write back. If not, I'll totally understand and wish you a happy life.*

*Best always,*
*Craig*

She clicks on the link and sees the story about Bottlecap. Some of the band names sound familiar, but only vaguely. She and Craig used to listen to a lot of music back then, but it was more his thing than hers. These days, she only listens to NPR.

Ashley clicks back to Craig's email. She's thought about him over the years—some movie or TV show reminding her of him—and whenever that happened she'd smile until her memories got swallowed up by how it ended. Because of this (because she knew how those memories would always end) she got very good at short-circuiting any thought of Craig—pushing it aside so that he would rarely, if ever, enter her mind.

Her hands hover over the laptop. She tries to weigh the pros and cons of responding.

*What could be the harm of writing back? What's the worst that could happen?*

She gets a reminder for the 4:00 PM meeting, fifteen minutes away. Ashley leans into her computer and quickly writes to Craig. She presses SEND.

After what seems like just a few seconds, she notices something in her inbox. It's from Craig.

It sends a shiver down her spine to know that he's out there, at that moment, thinking about her and writing the words that just appeared on her screen. It's almost as if they're having a conversation, their first in decades. She's breathing fast as she reads his response.

*Ash,*

*Thanks so much for writing back. After all this time I wasn't sure what you'd think of me or us or the time we shared. And I hope you don't mind my asking, but do you want to try and get together? Just to say hi? I'd love to hear about what you've been up to all of these years. What do you say? Lunch? Saturday?*

*Let me know.*

*C*

The reminder for her meeting pings again. She looks and can see it's 4:00 PM. She clicks on the small X in the corner of the pop-up window. She turns again to Craig's email, focusing on two words in particular. *Lunch. Saturday.* She can't remember ever having lunch with Craig. Not when they were dating, or even when they lived together.

*There's nothing more unsexy than lunch.*

So she writes back. *Yes. Okay. I'll meet you. Just let me know where and when.*

"Ashley, you coming?"

Heart still racing, she looks up and sees Bea standing in the doorway. She's holding a large present covered in Spider-Man wrapping paper.

"Jenna's baby shower, remember?"

Ashley remembers signing a card and contributing twenty dollars towards a Target gift card. She also remembers hoping she'd be busy when the day of the shower actually rolled around. It's bad enough that Margot was by yesterday with her infant.

"Of course," Ashley says. "Be right there."

Bea smiles, nods, and disappears down the hall, heading toward the break room. Ashley sits there for a second. She hears noise coming from the direction Bea just headed. She figures everyone's there, the shower has already started. Ashley slowly reaches to where her purse is sitting on the ground. She grabs it and places it on her desk. She closes her laptop and slides it into the purse. On the bottom of her purse she sees a few loose pills. They're yellow, triangular. Dylar. She stopped taking it a few months ago—too many side effects—preferring the Protraxanon. But she left the prescription bottle at home, so she fishes out a Dylar tablet and swallows it dry. She slings the purse over her shoulder and begins to tiptoe out of her office.

"Ashley? Where are you going?"

She looks up to see Jenna standing in the hallway, blocking what would have been a perfect escape. Sherry, the nosy receptionist, is in the break room with the others. Jenna's wearing a white cotton top stretched over her huge stomach. Ashley can see her belly button bulging out, practically the size of a doorknob.

"Oh, Jenna, hey. I just need to put a few things in my car." She points to her purse. "Laptop and—stuff. And then I'll be right back."

"Okay, well, hurry up or you're going to miss the games!"

Jenna smiles as she speaks. She practically glows. Ashley never really liked Jenna, but now she hates her. Jenna starts to walk down the hallway, one hand on her belly, exhaling in short breaths that sound like she's already gone into labor. Bea runs back into her office, coming out a second later holding a large sheet cake outlined with blue icing. The top of the cake reads IT'S A BOY. Jenna follows Bea into the conference room. The chatter of voices rises to a crescendo, everyone saying how great the cake looks, everyone saying how great Jenna looks. Sherry's voice rises above the others screaming, "Joy, joy, *joy!*"

Ashley tiptoes through the lobby, tiptoes out the door, gets into her Prius, and drives away.

Craig comes back from a late afternoon errand to discover that the office has been rearranged. Where his desk was this morning there's nothing but a keg and a box of red plastic cups. Underneath the window overlooking the parking lot, where there used to be a printer and a caddy full of office supplies, there are now bags of chips, pretzels, and cookies. In the kitchen the coffeemaker's been moved to make way for a margarita machine and someone—an intern, maybe—is filling the refrigerator with bottles of beer. Craig tries to remember if there's a party today or if they're celebrating something, or shipping a new version of the site, or if it's Steve Jobs's birthday, but nothing comes to mind. It could also just be that it's Wednesday.

Craig spots Josh in the corner, helping one of the coders move a Ping-Pong table into the conference room. Josh, wearing pool shoes with socks, baggy shorts, and a T-shirt that says HTML 5, catches Craig's eye and nods. Craig returns the nod and then continues to look for a place to sit.

Wandering through the office, Craig sees messenger bags, fixed-gear bikes, yoga balls, a case of tequila, but no desks. Finally, in the corner, where there used to be two whiteboards on casters, he finds six desks pushed up against a wall. Four of the desks are occupied by coders with headphones on, their fingers moving madly across their keyboards.

Craig's used to this. The layout of the office changes every couple of weeks. Sometimes there's a warning, sometimes it's a surprise. Josh thinks that it keeps everyone fresh and on their toes. Craig thinks that it's bad for morale and shows that Josh can't make up his mind about anything.

*I used to have an office. With windows, a view, two seats for guests. A little table. A radio. I used to have a door.*

Josh emerges from the conference room and sees Craig. He nods yet again before walking over.

"Thought we'd make a little change," Josh says. "You like?"

"Looking good. It's just, at first, I couldn't find where to sit and, you know, work."

"Matt was supposed to leave Post-its with people's names, but we let him go this morning." Josh sneers as he looks around the room. "It was the last thing he was supposed to do."

Craig doesn't even question Matt's departure. He's seen so many people come and go from Seatr that he's no longer shocked when it happens. Some days there are new people in the office, sitting at a desk and typing away. Some days Craig finds that the guy who'd been sitting across from him for the past two months has gone missing. Thinking back, he can't even remember what Matt looked like. Tall? Short? All that comes to mind is a laptop covered in stickers.

"Anyway, this area here . . ." Josh points to where a cluster of desks used to sit in the middle of the room, equidistant from the conference room, entrance, and other side of the office. "This is now an open space for stand-up meetings, or just to chill."

"Maybe yoga?"

Craig's joking, but Josh's eyes light up.

"*Now* you're thinking outside the box."

"And I see you put a Ping-Pong table in the conference room."

Josh's smile widens.

"Awesome, right? James even made a digital leaderboard with a ranking system. Keeps track of wins and losses."

"Sounds hardcore."

"Yeah, he's pretty into it." Josh leans in. When he does, Craig can smell Axe body spray. "Even brought his own paddle."

Craig looks over to James's desk. His chair's empty, his screen's blank. An elaborate wooden case sits open, revealing a lining of light-brown fur but no paddle.

"He even programmed the leaderboard so you can challenge other players. It's constantly updated and every player is ranked. You, by the way, are dead last."

Craig hears a game getting started. The ensuing volley is so fast that it sounds like a woodpecker.

"Yeah, sorry. It's just, I've been a little busy incorporating the feedback from the board meeting."

"Craig, you need to be a team player. Don't you see that? We're only as good as our weakest link and, right now, I'm afraid that's you."

"Because of . . . Ping-Pong?"

"Because of *attitude*."

Craig's body heats up and his face feels flush.

"Mobile marketing strategies are great and all," Josh continues, "but culture eats strategy for breakfast. Everybody knows that. And, well, there's a whole *culture* aspect to this job that I can't help but feel you're just not connecting with."

"Like?"

"Like you didn't go on the scavenger hunt last week. You never have a beer with us after work, and I can't help but notice that you declined the invitation for indoor skydiving."

"Oh, yeah, *that*. It's just, I have a root canal that day."

"And you'd rather do that than go indoor skydiving?"

*Yes. Absolutely.*

"No, not at all. It's just—I really need to get that done."

Out of the corner of his eye Craig sees James come out of the conference room. He has a smile on his face and sweat on his forehead. A few seconds later one of the coders comes out, his head hanging low. James puts the paddle back into its case with the care and caution you'd show a baby.

"As one of our senior employees," Josh is saying, "I really expect you to take the lead."

He hopes that when Josh says *senior* he's connoting status or stature, but Craig can't help but think that Josh just means *old*.

"Lead?"

"You know, be an example for some of the younger staffers."

Craig takes a deep breath.

"You're right, Josh. It's my fault. I'll try harder."

"Good. Oh, by the way, we've got a little trouble with TSA. Apparently they think our plan of having people stand in for other people at airports might hamper national security. They're afraid terrorists, or people on no-fly lists, are going to buy someone else's ticket as a way of getting on a plane. They say we're violating federal law. Patriot Act. Blah-blah-blah."

"Well, that's sort of our business model," Craig says. "What do we do?"

"Don't worry about it. I know a senator."

"You do?"

"From Obama's first campaign. I worked on the website. He's a good guy, by the way. Anyway, I can get the senator to make a few calls. I set up his Twitter account, so he owes me."

He begins to walk away, but Craig calls out to him.

"By the way, Josh?"

"Yeah?"

"The Ping-Pong table. Where are we supposed to have meetings?"

"I don't follow."

"The conference room. That's where we have board meetings. It's where we do product reviews and Q&A testing with focus groups. Now it's the Ping-Pong room."

Josh just grins and turns around. As he crosses the office, he says, "Craig, you think too much."

Craig digs his laptop out of his bag. He chooses one of the two free desks, pulls up a chair, and sits down.

He opens his laptop, looking for an email from Ashley. As he scans through all of his various messages—Facebook updates, newsletters, spam—he sees it.

*She wrote back.*

Trembling, his hand clicks on the email. Her message appears on his screen.

*Craig,*

*Thanks for reaching out, and thanks for the link about the Bottlecap show. That brought back lots of memories for me, too. Some of them good ones ;-)*

*I've of course thought about you over the years, wondering where you are and how you're doing. So it's nice to hear from you. Thanks for reaching out.*

*Feel free to write again sometime.*

Craig feels warm.

*It wasn't all forgotten.*

He now knows that he'll always be a part of her, like a fossil trapped miles below the surface of the earth. A creature who lived and who died and who left an imprint of his body inside of hers. You can never get rid of the people you've known, even if you no longer know them.

He hits REPLY and writes back a short note, asking her to lunch this weekend. He figures she'll probably say no, but it's worth a shot. He's about to get back to work, putting on his headphones to drown out the latest Ping-Pong game that's just started, when he sees that Ashley's already replied. He clicks on the email.

*Yes. Okay. I'll meet you. Just let me know where and when.*

He's about to respond when something on his laptop makes a noise. It's a notice from some program, but Craig's not sure which one. Has he been tagged in a photo? Has someone sent him a message? He spots a window in the upper corner that features a skull and crossbones, the words YOU HAVE BEEN CHALLENGED flashing underneath in big red letters. Craig clicks on the window and he's taken to a website called The Seatr Open. A chiptune version of Chopin's funeral march begins playing while, at the top of the screen, an animated ball is whacked back and forth by digital paddles at opposite ends of the screen.

Craig looks and can see all of Seatr's staffers ranked, with a calendar showing future matches as well as columns for wins and losses. There's even a chat room where the coders are talking trash. Names he doesn't recognize are ranked well ahead of him. Matt, the guy fired this morning, was in third place. Next to Craig's name is a smaller version of the skull and crossbones he saw earlier. Underneath, it says CHALLENGED. When Craig clicks on it another window appears.

*James has challenged you to an epic battle on May 14th at 2:00 PM. What say you? Accept or admit defeat? Decide!*

Craig just sighs.

*For fuck's sake. What does this have to do with reselling airline tickets?*

Craig turns and sees James staring at him. The music coming out of James's headphones sounds like jackhammers and dental equipment. Craig notices for the first time a number of tattoos—wild colors swirling around bulging biceps—peeking out from under the sleeves of the same HTML 5 T-shirt that Josh is wearing. Craig hears James grunt, and this makes him gulp.

Craig turns back to his laptop. He hits ACCEPT.

Ashley wakes up to smells. Good smells, not like when the sewer line to the house next door broke and sent raw sewage rushing into the street. Or when the garbage disposal stopped working and the smell of rotting food filled the house for days.

*Maple?*

She's barely awake.

*Coffee?*

Ashley pushes the covers down and sees that she's wearing a pair of Andrew's sweatpants. She rolls out of bed, lets out a big yawn, grabs a yellow terrycloth robe from the slipper chair. She heads downstairs.

Placing her hand in the pocket of her robe, Ashley feels plastic. She pulls it out. It's the prescription bottle. The date's from only two weeks ago, but the bottle's almost empty. It was supposed to last for months. She unscrews the top and lifts the amber bottle to her lips, tipping one into her mouth. The pill's coating is sweet as she swallows.

Ashley enters the kitchen and sees Andrew at the stove. It's covered with pans emitting wonderful smells. Underneath the pans she can see blue flames dancing from the constant draft that runs through the house.

"Morning," Andrew says. He's wearing khakis and a patterned shirt. His hair is combed. In addition to the breakfast smells filling the room, she can smell him. Aftershave and cologne.

"You teaching today?"

"Of course, sweetheart. But I thought I'd get up early and make us some breakfast. Hope I didn't wake you."

Ashley lies and says no. Most days begin with a lie. Andrew will ask, "Did you sleep well? Did you have any bad dreams?" And her answers of yes and no are always lies.

"Good, then sit down. I made pancakes and turkey sausage and heated up the maple syrup we bought in New Hampshire. The expensive stuff that comes in those little paint cans. And, of course, there's coffee."

As she moves across the kitchen to fill up her cup, Ashley says "coffee" the way zombies in movies say "brains." It overflows and burns her hand. The spot where it splashed is red and raised. Ashley sucks on it, tasting first coffee and then her flesh.

Andrew pulls out a chair for her and points.

"You just sit down. I'll bring you everything you need."

When she sits, he pushes in her chair and goes back to the stove, flipping a pancake and rotating the sausages. Andrew lifts a lid on a small saucepan to make sure the syrup's not boiling over. As he does this he hums the theme to *This American Life*. She hates it when he's like this, hates it when he's tender.

He goes to the refrigerator and pulls out a huge container of orange juice. It's double the size she usually buys. The package is covered with drawings of oranges and a smiling cartoon sun wearing sunglasses. At the top, underneath NO PULP, it says FAMILY SIZE. She's told him not to buy these. No big boxes of Frosted Flakes, no huge jars of mayonnaise. No double-packs of potato chips. Whenever she looks into the refrigerator or pantry and sees these things, it breaks her heart. When he asked her why, after the first time, she yelled at him for bringing home a family-sized box of cookies, all she said—under her breath—was, "We're not a family."

Andrew puts a plate of food in front of Ashley and goes back to the stove to prepare one for himself. She picks up her knife and fork and pushes the food around the plate, chopping it up and moving it from side to side to make it look like it's disappearing. It's the same trick she used when she was a kid. Andrew joins her at the table.

"Ashley, your food. Eat. Eat."

She picks at her pieces of pancake and sausage, taking little sips of juice and big gulps of coffee. She finds the digital clock on the microwave and sees it's almost eight. In an hour she'll be at the office. Right now is as peaceful as her day gets, but she doesn't feel very peaceful.

While taking a sip of coffee, she thinks about the weekend and lunch with Craig. She knows she has to come up with some story, some excuse to tell Andrew. Some way to justify being out of the house.

"What's on your mind, babe?"

"What?"

"You seem a million miles away."

"Oh," Ashley says. "It's just—this weekend."

"What about it?"

He takes a big bite of his pancakes. Syrup dribbles down his chin until he wipes it off with a paper towel that leaves white cotton specks in his stubble.

"I have to go shopping on Saturday."

Ashley knows that Andrew hates going shopping. He'll consider it a privilege to not be involved.

"Oh, really? What for?"

Ashley hadn't expected him to go down another layer.

"Oh, well, you remember Jenna? From work?"

"The one that's pregnant?"

"Yes."

"What about her?"

"Well, I just figured I should get her something."

Andrew takes a long sip of his coffee.

"But I thought you hated her."

"No, she's—nice."

"That's not why you hated her."

"Andrew, please." Her voice rises. "Give me a little bit of credit. I can be happy for someone, can't I?"

"But—didn't you already get her something?"

"What?"

"You had a shower at work. Didn't you contribute some money toward a gift card? Target, I think. You told me about it a few weeks ago."

*That's the kind of thing he remembers? I hate him.*

"Yeah, but that's kind of impersonal, don't you think? I thought I ought to, you know, pick something out myself. Make it more heartfelt."

"So, where will you go?"

"I guess I'll go out to that Babies R Us near the mall."

Ashley figures she can run out there tomorrow on her lunch hour, get a little something and stash it in her trunk. On Saturday, when she returns from her lunch with Craig, she'll bring Jenna's present into the house and show it to Andrew as proof of her lie.

"Well, do you want some company? I was going to drive out to the library to do some research on Saturday afternoon, but I could push that to next week if you need some moral support."

"Moral support? God, Andrew, will you listen to yourself?"

"I'm sorry, Ashley—I'm just trying to help. I know that you—"

"Look, it's *fine*. I can go by myself. I'm a big girl, okay?"

Andrew pushes away his plate. Neither of them has eaten much. Ashley suddenly thinks of something.

*The receipt. What if he looks at the receipt? It'll say Friday and not Saturday. Well, I'll just go on Saturday, on my way to see Craig. That way everything will match up.*

"You do whatever you need to do, okay?" Andrew's voice shakes when he speaks.

Ashley sees the bags under his eyes. She tries to remember what he looked like when they first met. Was he dashing? Was he handsome? All she knows is that he didn't look like this.

"I've got to go."

Andrew gets up. He takes his plate and drops it into the sink. It falls with a clatter. Ashley continues to stare into her pancakes.

"Leave the dishes," he says. "I'll do them when I get home tonight. See you then, okay?"

"Okay."

After he disappears from the kitchen, Ashley tracks his movements through the house. She can hear him grab a jacket from the coatrack in the hallway, scoop his car keys out of the bowl on the end table near the stairs, fetch the backpack full of books from where it's hanging on the series of hooks lining the wall opposite the staircase. The door opens and then closes. Seconds go by. Andrew's car starts up and then is gone.

After he leaves, Ashley hears other cars in the street go by. The morning commute has begun. She figures she'd better take a shower and join in. She starts to get up, but stops. She feels tingly, slightly numb, the Protraxanon kicking in. She sits back down and, for a few seconds, forgets the shower and getting dressed. She forgets about work, Andrew, Craig, everything. She looks down at her hand and sees the burn from before, from the coffee. She rubs it, puzzled. It no longer hurts.

Craig's alone on the shuttle. It's something Seatr started a few weeks ago, chartering a small bus to ferry employees back and forth from the office to a few points in downtown Kitty as well as a carpool lot near I-95 where the Waffle House used to be. The shuttle can fit twenty people, and has reclining leather seats with footrests and cup-holders. There's Wi-Fi and even a bathroom.

The idea is employees will take the shuttle instead of driving, be able to relax or do work while they're transported to the office in style. Josh hoped it'd be a perk to make Seatr more attractive to prospective employees, as well as keeping the ones they already have happy. Besides, it's the kind of thing the big companies do out in Silicon Valley. But since Craig only lives ten minutes from the office, he usually just drives. This is his first time on the shuttle. After his talk with Josh yesterday, he figured he'd better start showing more team spirit.

By the time the shuttle drops him off, it's ten o'clock and the office is almost full. There's also a Ping-Pong game going in the conference room.

Josh and the head of product are huddled around a whiteboard in the far corner. Josh has a marker in his left hand. On the whiteboard are a bunch of letters, numbers, and mathematical symbols. The head of product is saying, "Josh, this is brilliant. I wish I'd thought of that. How do you do it? *Totally* amazing." Craig wishes he were on the same wavelength as everyone else in the office. He wishes he were in on the secret.

Upon finding his new desk, Craig discovers his chair's been replaced by a blue yoga ball. He sighs and sits down, almost falling over at first. On either side coders sit wearing headphones, thumping bass seeping out as their fingers move rhythmically over their keyboards. In the kitchen more coders, along with a few board members, are talking about which credit cards give the best rewards. A board member is saying something about blackout days, while a coder—Craig's not sure of his name—keeps insisting that Discover's the best. "They had all that stuff years ago," he insists. "They just didn't brand it well." The board member just rolls his eyes and says, "Don't you get it? Branding is *everything*."

Craig opens his laptop. Josh sent him half a dozen emails last night about various things he wants Craig to tackle by the end of the week. Rewriting their welcome emails, starting a newsletter, getting an RFP on a CRM system so they can start a Seatr loyalty program. The emails were sent starting at one in the morning and continued until almost four, one every half hour or so.

Despite everything he has to do, Craig decides to do some research for his lunch this weekend.

He hadn't meant to try and get together with Ashley—at least not yet. He figured they'd trade emails for a while and, a few weeks later—after reestablishing a rapport, becoming a presence in her life—he'd suggest a phone call. From there they'd move on to texting, and only then would he suggest some sort of meeting. He thought it'd be drinks or, if he was brash, dinner. But lunch on a Saturday? He doesn't know what came over him except he was excited to think of her out there thinking about him, so he came up with a way to see her sooner rather than later.

He opens a Word doc and types the names of all the restaurants he knows in and around Kitty. He then goes through the list—visiting their websites, looking them up on Yelp—trying to see if one's suitable for Saturday. One by one he decides against them.

*Too fancy. Too casual. Too public.*

He decides this is all crazy since he doesn't really know what this lunch is. He's searched for more information about Ashley online, to see if she's married or divorced or has kids or what, but all he can find is her LinkedIn profile. Without any more information he doesn't know if this is a date or just a casual get-together, doesn't know if this is closure or some sort of new beginning.

After going through the list a second time, he decides on Nolan's. It's nice and takes reservations, comfortable without being overtly romantic. He grabs his phone and goes into the hallway to make a reservation. As he passes the coders in the kitchen, he can hear them talking about Bitcoin.

"Hello, Nolan's." The woman's voice is perky. "How can I help you?"

Craig makes a reservation for noon on Saturday. He sends a quick email to Ashley telling her the location and the time. After he presses SEND his heart starts to race.

Heading back into Seatr, he sees Josh standing near his desk. Josh is wearing brown cargo shorts, blue Toms, and a bright green T-shirt that says WHO'S YOUR DATA? As Craig passes the group of coders, he can hear they're now talking about Space X.

"Craig, my man. Pretty nice, eh?"

"Nice?"

"I understand you took the shuttle this morning."

"Oh, yeah." Craig sits down, wobbling for a second on the ball. "It was nice all right. I was the only one on it."

"Well, it's early days."

"But most of these guys don't even drive." Craig nods toward the area near the windows, where he used to sit. It's now filled with bikes. Now the bikes have the view. "The coders all live in the new condos down the street. Some of them even walk to work. The shuttle probably drives right past them."

"We're growing, Craig. *Growing*. I'm the CEO, remember? I'm trying to think two moves ahead."

"But the money it must have cost to—"

Josh interrupts him.

"Craig, you need to trust me. I've done this before, okay?"

"Okay, Josh. It's just—the site's still not making any money and I'm worried that we're going to—"

Josh puts his hands on Craig's shoulders. His grip is firm, his strength impressive. Craig looks at Josh's face. He's lean and tan and there's not a wrinkle on him. Josh says, again, "*Trust* me."

Craig replies, dreamily, "I trust you."

Josh removes his grip, his arms falling back to his side. Craig shakes off the trance he'd momentarily fallen into.

"By the way," Josh says. "I don't want to make a big deal about it, but I noticed you didn't use your laptop."

"What?"

The Ping-Pong game ends with clapping and cheers. James exits the conference room triumphantly, arms raised. A few seconds later a board member shuffles out, his eyes glued to the carpet.

"On the shuttle ride," Josh says. "Just now. You didn't use your laptop."

"Oh, I was just relaxing and—wait, how did you know?"

"Server logs from the Wi-Fi."

"That can tell whether or not I was working?"

Josh shrugs.

"Not exactly. It can only tell whether or not you were accessing the network."

"So what if I was just using Excel or something?"

"We can tell that, too—but not until later. There's a program on all the company laptops that records your keystrokes, but that only syncs once a day."

Craig just sits there, balanced precariously on the yoga ball. In the conference room someone's started another game of Ping-Pong. Different bits of music seep out of various headphones and a guy in the corner—Josh described him last week to Craig as a "brand evangelist"—is wearing nothing but swim trunks as he watches *Breaking Bad* on an iPad.

"Look, about the shuttle," Josh says. "It's no big deal. Really. Next time, just—you know—try a little harder. We all have a lot to do around here."

"I will, Josh. Speaking of which, I got your emails last night. When do you ever sleep?"

"What? Oh, *that.*" He leans in again. "That wasn't me."

"How do you mean?"

"I really wasn't up. Well, at least not *working.* I was with Alex, a girl I met at the tech meetup. We went back to her place. She works for Pillw and, well, let's just say a few pillows were *indeed* involved, if you know what I mean."

"But—the emails."

"That's just an app called Schedulr. You preload in a bunch of emails and tell it when to send them. It plugs right into your email. To the person getting the email, it looks like it was sent at two in the morning or whatever."

"But why? What's point?"

"Motivation," Josh says. "Team building. If everyone thinks I'm working nonstop, it'll inspire them to do the same and, in just a few months, we'll have a world-class product on our hands."

"But why are you telling me this? Now I know it's not really you."

"I don't know, Craig. You're different." He waves his hands around the room. "For a lot of these guys it's their first job. But you—you're *seasoned.*"

The word sinks in.

"Just get to that stuff when you can, okay? If we get our act together we can grab some of the summer travel action. I have a friend at the *Daily Beast.*"

"You do?"

"Yeah, Tina Brown. I built the *New Yorker*'s database. Anyway, she'll run a feature on us if we can make it worth their while."

"But the site's still not working."

"Craig. *Craig*. What did I just say? *Trust* me."

Josh's hands are placed again on Craig's shoulders.

Craig says, slowly, "I trust you."

Mark pulls up to the Dark Star Lounge. He parks alongside the building, forgetting at first to lock the rental car. He backtracks a few steps and hits the button on the keychain. The horn squeaks, the headlights blink.

As he walks around to the club's entrance, he can't believe how big the building is. It's long and low and takes up pretty much the entire block. A sign above the entrance says NO REENTRY WITHOUT HANDSTAMP. As he approaches the large double doors Mark starts to get nervous. He's not sure there are enough Bottlecap fans in town, let alone the world, to fill a building this large.

Dark Star doesn't open until seven, but he's meeting the writer for a drink at five. Mark checks his phone. 4:56. He knocks on the door. While he waits for someone to answer, he notices a framed calendar of events next to the box office. For the month of May, besides Bottlecap and the other groups playing next Saturday, Mark doesn't see any bands. There are just things like: IT'S A SIN, '80s DJ NIGHT, and GOTH ANTHEMS WITH MC BROOD. Also, Wednesday is ladies' night.

A guy finally opens one of the doors. He's wearing a black T-shirt that says STAFF tucked into his jeans.

"You Mark?"

Mark nods.

"My manager told me you'd be by. Come on in."

Mark steps into the club.

Closing the door, the guy says, "Feel free to look around. If you need anything, my name's Rick."

Mark nods again as Rick wanders off, disappearing behind a door marked EMPLOYEES ONLY. The inside of the club is mostly dark. Mark sees a few lights on here and there, along with shadowy bodies

71

sweeping the floor and stocking a bar at the back of a long room at the front of which is a stage. Mark walks up to the edge of the stage. It's bigger than any of the clubs he used to play with Bottlecap. Back then they never played to more than 350 people at a time, but the Dark Star Lounge looks to fit maybe twice that. The stage has big monitors and huge speakers suspended from the ceiling on both sides of the stage, strung together to form a big C. Dozens of lights stick out from black scaffolding above and behind the stage, the differently colored gels seem bright even in the darkness. And in the middle of the room, hoisted above the floor, is a disco ball.

Mark gulps and walks back to the bar. He catches the attention of a Hispanic-looking guy bringing in cases of Rolling Rock.

"Can I just get a club soda or something?"

The guy fills up a glass from a pistol-shaped dispenser, puts it on the bar, and walks away. Mark sits down, his back to the stage. He can't bear to look at it, to imagine himself up there playing guitar and singing. It's been so long.

After he left the band, Mark hung around LA for a while, writing new songs, recording demos, trying to get another band together. When the Bottlecap record finally came out—after Gary and Steve had found another guy to play guitar and sing—there were magazine and newspaper stories about Mark here and there. Writers wanted to talk to the ex–lead singer of the hot new band and get his side of the story. Why did he do it? Why did he walk out on fame and fortune? Mark hated the questions because he didn't have good answers. He usually tried to pass it off as artistic purity. He didn't want his music watered down, didn't want to play the major label game. The word "vision" was used so often you would have thought he was an ophthalmologist. It usually worked. Rock and roll has a long line of misunderstood geniuses who walked away from their careers in one form or another: Syd Barrett, Lee Mavers, and now Mark Pellion.

Even though the band had a bit of success without him—Lollapalooza, a Buzz Bin video on *120 Minutes*, the cover of *Alternative Press*—it didn't take long for their star to fall. Bottlecap was eventually dropped by the label and the singer who'd replaced Mark left for a solo career. Steve and Gary, not wanting to draft yet another guy to sing and play guitar, broke up Bottlecap, retired the name, and moved back to Kitty. Just a few years after the adventure began, it ended.

"You Mark?"

He turns to see a young guy wearing a T-shirt and skinny jeans walking towards him from the entrance.

"Yeah, you Seth?"

Seth nods and they shake hands. Seth hops onto a barstool and pulls an iPhone out of his pocket, placing it on the bar.

"Okay to record this? I'll transcribe it later."

Mark shrugs.

The same guy from before appears with more cases of beer. Seth asks for a Diet Coke.

"I don't know how much your label guy Dave told you," Seth begins, "but I'd love to do a story about the show next week about all the bands coming back to town and where you guys are now. Is that cool?"

Mark shrugs again. Seth takes a sip of the Diet Coke, punches some buttons on his iPhone. Mark waits for him to take out a notebook or a piece of paper. Instead, Seth just starts asking questions.

"So, tell me about the show next week."

"Yeah," Mark says, "the show . . ."

For a few seconds, he draws a blank. What's he supposed to say? He kicks himself for not syncing with Dave. Should he talk about the label? Is he supposed to hype the concert, or the other bands? After taking a sip of his club soda in order to stall, he finally mumbles something about it being an honor to get the group back together again and how he's looking forward to playing for a hometown crowd. When he stops talking, Seth gives him an approving look and Mark relaxes.

"You know," Seth says, "you're the first band we've had here in a while. Normally it's just DJs. There's now a trivia night, and on Tuesdays there are comedians." Seth looks around the cavernous space, and then points at the floor in front of the stage. "Things got so slow for a while, they did yoga right there twice a week."

"Why don't any bands play here? I know Kitty's small, but there's got to be some kind of scene."

Mark thinks back to when he lived here. In addition to Bottlecap, there were half a dozen bands in town. They played shows together, shared gear, had feuds, and swapped members as well as girlfriends. Dave had most of these bands on his label for a seven-inch or on a compilation, if not putting out a full-length album. Out of all of them, Bottlecap was the only one to get some type of recognition outside of Kitty, or even outside of Virginia. No one else from town ever got signed.

"Scene?" Seth laughs. "Those are *gone*."

"Yeah, but—"

Seth cuts him off.

"What, you're thinking of something like New York City in the seventies? Athens in the eighties? That kind of thing doesn't exist anymore. It doesn't need to. Scenes are just a room in Reddit, or a tag in Bandcamp. And those are places I can go to on my computer." Seth points to the bar. "Hell, I can go there on my *phone*."

Mark's own phone buzzes. He looks down. It's a text from Gary with the address of the practice space where they're all meeting on Saturday.

Seth points. "Do you need to answer that?"

Mark turns the phone over.

"No, it's nothing. Keep going."

"It's just—there's nothing I can't get online."

"Yeah, but what about going to concerts? Having firsthand experiences? Being in a crowd?"

"I did a road trip out to Coachella and it was ridiculous. I'd never seen more rich kids staring at their phones." Seth laughs. "If I'd wanted to sit in a field and constantly check Facebook and Instagram, I could have just stayed home."

"I don't know." Mark slouches on the barstool. He takes a sip of the club soda, now turned room temperature. "Maybe you're right."

After a few more questions, Seth declares that he has all he needs. They both get up, leaving their empty glasses on the bar. The door's locked again, and they have to shout to get someone to let them out. While they're waiting, Seth fiddles with his phone while Mark just stares down at his sneakers. Finally, a different guy also wearing a STAFF T-shirt opens the door.

As they exit the club both of them blink as their eyes adjust to the light. There's still only Mark's rental car parked beside the building. Seth stands there, looking around.

Mark asks, "Do you need a ride?"

"Nah," Seth waves him off. "I'm waiting for an Uber."

Mark gasps.

"What, you guys have Uber down here, too?"

"Yeah," Seth grins. "Running water, too."

Charles wears sunglasses to the office, hoping to hide the bags under his eyes. He didn't sleep at all last night. All Charles could think about was the roof, and where he's going to get the money to pay for it. It didn't help that he was lying there, staring at the ceiling. In the half-dark of the room—the hallway's nightlight casting shadows across their floor and one of the walls—Charles looked for wet spots and stains in the plaster above his head. All he found were streaks of paint and shadows. He sniffed again for mold in the air, but all he could smell was the lotion Grace puts on her face, hands, and elbows every night before she goes to sleep.

Now, after fighting to stay awake during his morning commute, Charles sleepwalks into the small kitchen on the twelfth floor. He's headed for the coffee he desperately needs to stay awake. Brooks enters, notices the sunglasses, and asks, "Late night last night?"

Charles winks and says, "You know it." He immediately realizes the wink is lost on Brooks because of the sunglasses. But since it's just Brooks, Charles doesn't worry about it.

He grabs a mug from the cupboard and fills it up, topping it off with cream and sugar. He walks away, leaving splashes of milk and a sprinkling of sugar on the counter.

Charles goes to his office, closes the door, sips his coffee, and tries to get ready for his meeting with Tom. He tries to think of some small talk, as well as office gossip, to get the conversation started. Since he's really not sure what the chat will be about, he doesn't know what else to prepare. For a second he thinks it might be about what Brooks said at the meeting the other day, his report on sales projections. But Charles doesn't think so. That could be handled with a quick email written by his assistant. Tom wouldn't schedule a meeting just for that.

When it's finally time to go upstairs, Charles slowly rises from his desk and walks down the hallway. Before heading to the elevator, he stops by the bathroom. He relieves himself of the coffee and then rinses out his mouth so he doesn't have coffee breath. As he's leaving, Dylan enters and gives him a smirk.

*Fucking idiot.*

Upstairs, Heather asks him to have a seat. Charles obliges, sitting and crossing his legs in what he hopes is a masculine way. As the seconds turn into minutes, and the minutes begin to stack up, he tries not to let his mind wander. Charles tries to stay focused, but fatigue begins to catch up with him. Any lift he'd been given by the caffeine fades. His stomach, at first just grumbling, begins to do flips. He tries to take his mind off the waiting by pulling out his iPhone and checking his email. He figures if Tom walks up and sees him on his phone, it'll make him look dedicated, a workaholic.

He quickly responds to a few emails and texts. Then he sees Randy's email from the other day about that concert next week. When Charles mentioned him to Grace again last night, lamenting that they'd drifted out of touch and talking about what great friends they used to be, she suggested having Randy over for dinner this weekend. Charles writes a quick email.

*Randy, hey. Yeah, the Bottlecap thing sounds great, but we'd also like you to come to dinner on Saturday if you're up for it. Just let me know.*

As he hits SEND he sees Tom approaching from the direction of O'Brien's office.

"Charles, my man." Tom slaps Charles on the knee. "Hope you weren't waiting long."

"Not at all. Just got here."

Heather shoots Charles a look.

"Then come on in." Tom enters his office. While Charles gets up and follows him, Tom calls out, "Heather, darling, hold my calls, will you?"

As he closes the door, Tom motions for Charles to take a seat. Charles approaches the chair but hovers near it for a moment, waiting for Tom to sit down first. Charles catches a slight grin on Tom's face as he does this.

"So, Charles, how are you?"

"Good, good."

"How's Maddie? What is she, six now?"

"Eight, actually."

"Eight? Wow. Time flies."

"And how're your boys?"

Charles knows that Tom has two boys, thirteen and two.

"An adventure, always an adventure."

Then there's silence. Charles wonders whether he should try and fill it. Should he make the comment about the weather he'd come up with earlier? He decides it's Tom's move.

"Listen," Tom finally says. "Thanks for coming by. As you know, there's been a lot of scuttlebutt about some changes and reorgs and everything and, well, I just wanted to make sure you heard this straight from me."

"Of course," Charles says. He crosses his legs and leans back, trying to look comfortable, even though he's not.

"The fact of the matter is, we're going to make Dylan a vice president. He'll be moving up here to work directly with the management team. I wanted to tell you personally because it means you'll be taking on a few of his former duties."

Charles is stunned. He's not sure he heard it right, the name *Dylan* and not *Charles*. His phone buzzes in his pocket, probably a text from Grace with an even more expensive quote from the contractor.

"Well, Tom." Charles's voice is even and measured even though his heart is racing and he's pissed off. "I have to admit, this is a bit of a shock."

Tom looks down and makes circles on the glass desktop with his palm. Charles sees that Tom's wedding band is tight around his ring finger. It's practically cutting into his skin. Charles hopes it hurts.

"I know, I know." Tom's shaking his head. "To be honest, it was a shock to me, too. And, not to pass the buck, but this isn't a decision I feel I can agree with wholeheartedly."

"You mean because Dylan's a fucking idiot?"

Tom laughs. Cursing in the office is not only accepted, it's encouraged. If you can't say "fuck," you'll never rise above assistant.

"I appreciate your candor," Tom says, "and I want you to know your feelings are echoed among some of the management team."

There's silence again. Charles fears that Tom is going to leave it there, with indignation registered but no change in the actual decision. That's not good enough. Charles wants that job. He *needs* that job.

"You know that Dylan's intern does most of his work, don't you?"

"What?"

"Sharon," Charles says, not quite believing he's saying it. "Well, she's not exactly an intern, but she might as well be. Isn't even a *manager*. She does everything. If you want to make someone VP, promote *her*."

Tom chuckles darkly. The only women you see on the sixteenth floor are secretaries. He slowly says, "Continue."

"She writes all of his reports, does the weekly highlights email. She even pulls together the material for the newsletter every month. She also writes his presentations for the sales conference."

"You mean drafts, right? From his notes?"

"No, Tom. I mean the whole *fucking* thing. Frankly, Dylan doesn't have an original thought in his head. He's just taking up space. Everybody thinks so."

"Jesus."

"All Dylan does is say *yes yes yes* to whatever Sharon puts in front of him. Rubber-Stamp Stevens, that's what we call him."

They don't actually call him that, but it sounds good so Charles says it. All he's thinking about is his roof. And Maddie sleeping under the growing mold. Spores and germs and bacteria infecting his little girl, doing God only knows what to her developing brain.

"You are aware," Tom says, "of how highly O'Brien thinks of him."

This is the biggest stumbling block. Around Trust Insurance—around this branch, anyway—O'Brien is God. If tomorrow he sent around an email saying two plus two equals five, not only would everyone believe it, they'd make it their screensaver.

"I know that there's a connection between them, yes."

"Connection?!" Tom laughs. "He's like his goddamn nephew or something. How do you think that little shit got the job in the first place? The point is, O'Brien likes him."

There's silence again, but Charles doesn't know what to say to break it. What to offer, or how low he's willing to go. He needs Tom to take the lead.

"To be honest, Charles, I really didn't think you'd react this way. But I'm glad to hear it. You've got fire in your belly." Tom swivels in his chair and looks out the window. Charles looks out the window, too. The views from sixteen really are nice. Tom says, dreamily, "You remind me of me at your age."

Charles decides to go for it.

"Can it be stopped?"

Tom turns back to Charles.

"That depends."

"On what?"

"On what you can get me on Dylan." Tom leans forward, interlaces his fingers, and begins to whisper even though his door is closed and there's no way anyone could overhear their conversation. "If I'm going to go to O'Brien and try to kill this, I need proof. Some ammunition. O'Brien's going to push back, and I need to be prepared when he does."

Silence again. Out in the hall Charles can hear the pinging sound of the elevator arrive and its doors opening and closing. He says, "I think I can get you what you need."

"Well, okay then. See what you can dig up and, in the meantime, I'll tell O'Brien about our little discussion. Test the water a bit. Okay?"

"Okay."

Tom turns to his computer. Charles takes this to mean the meeting is over. He gets up and starts heading for the door. He's almost there when Tom speaks again.

"And I suppose that if Dylan doesn't get that job, *you'd* want it?"

Charles doesn't want to overplay his hand.

"Let's cross that bridge when we come to it."

Tom laughs.

"Fucking bullshitter. I love it."


Bookstorage is busy. All afternoon Randy's been running between the aisles carrying stack after stack of books, trading out the remainders for the new releases, restocking the Bestsellers section, and unpacking a box of children's books he should have unpacked last week. Hector's at checkout, Susan's behind the information desk, and Bill has been on everyone's ass all day, roaming the floor and telling the Bookstorage staffers to "look alive" over and over again.

As Randy digs out a few copies of a hefty new novel from a cardboard box that says RODNEY & CO. on the side, three women brush past him heading from Photography to Art. Randy begins placing the unboxed books on the shelf—some new novel with a lurid cover featuring vampires at the United Nations—just as a young couple come in. They're followed soon after by a woman with two kids. Susan looks up something on the computer for one of the art-book ladies while Bill helps Hector at the front desk with gift-wrapping. Randy expects all this on a weekend, but it's rare for a Thursday.

As he bends over for another handful of fiction, the phone in his back pocket buzzes. Bookstorage policy is to only make or receive calls, or read or send emails and texts, during designated break periods or before and after shifts while in the break room. But Randy figures *fuck it*, and heads to the back of the store. Crouching in Science Fiction, he checks his BlackBerry.

Charles has finally gotten back to him, agreeing to go to the concert but also inviting him to dinner this weekend. Randy writes back.

*Sounds good. Send me the deets when you can and I'll see you then.*

After sending the message, Randy looks up and sees Bill watching him from a few feet away. He's carrying a roll of James Joyce wrapping paper.

"When you're done with your personal correspondence, Randy, would you kindly meet me in my office? I'd like to have a word."

Bill brushes past him and heads toward his office, located just past the employee break room, on the other side of Self-Help. Randy can see Hector grinning at him from behind the cash register.

Randy slinks through the back of the store and finds the office door open. Bill's sitting behind a desk cluttered with invoices and packing slips. Randy's been in here a lot lately, getting lectures or a slap on the wrist for some silly violation like being late or chewing gum. It always feels like being sent to the principal's office.

Randy sits down and points to the wall. "Quite a crowd out there." On the other side of the wall is the store, where presumably there are still half a dozen people shopping for books.

"That's not a crowd, Randy. That's a few people killing time before their movie starts at the mall. They'd have to buy half the store every week to get this location out of the hole it's in. But that's not why I called you in here." Bill leans forward and places his elbows on the desk. He inhales deeply before speaking again. "I'm sure you're fully aware of Bookstorage policy—policy that I have now had to speak to you about on several occasions—about employee behavior. Well, this is going to be the last time."

When Bill stops talking, Randy wonders if he's supposed to say something. Apologize or admit something that Bill knows but that Randy doesn't think he knows.

"What are you saying, exactly?"

"I'm saying your services are no longer needed at Bookstorage. You're being let go. Today's your last day." Bill lets this soak in before continuing. "I was going to wait until closing, but your little stunt just now forced my hand. Turn in your vest and clock out."

"Bill, please." Randy's voice shakes when he speaks. He looks behind him at the open door. He wishes he had shut it. He doesn't want Hector or Susan to hear what he's about to say. "I know I've been remiss. And I'm sorry. But I like this job. I *need* this job. Please don't do this. *Please.*"

As Randy says this, Bill just looks over Randy's head. He refuses to make eye contact. Randy feels like an animal.

"Bill—"

But he's suddenly cut off.

"Randy, I'm sorry. You were a good employee once, but your heart's not in it anymore. Don't try and lie and tell me that it is. You come in late and you leave early. It's clear you don't want to be here. Hector and the others, well, they just have more—"

Bill stops speaking. He shuffles some papers on his desk, looking for the script. He continues. "It's been nice knowing you, and we wish you all of the success in the world. Thank you for all of the contributions you've made to the Bookstorage family." Bill says this in an emotionless way, like flight attendants going over safety procedures.

"Bill, I'm *begging* you. Don't do this."

Bill gets up, but stares at the ground. "Randy," he says, "I'm going to have to ask you to leave."

Randy doesn't move. But he doesn't really know what else to do, what else to say. When he finally stands up, his legs feel unsteady and his head feels light. It's all he can do to shuffle out of Bill's office. In the break room he peels off his Bookstorage vest and nametag, letting both drop to the floor. Randy's aware of Bill's presence behind him.

*He's probably making sure I don't steal anything on the way out. Like what? The water cooler? The packets of cream and sugar?*

As Randy's standing there, too stunned to move, Hector enters the break room. He says to Bill, "Mr. Fuller, we're running low on change. I thought I'd have Susan cover the front desk while I run to the bank before the evening rush. I don't think we can wait until tomorrow morning. I hope that's okay."

"Thanks, Hector." Bill nods approvingly. "That's smart thinking."

Hector walks back out to the floor. When the door's open, Randy sees shoppers lined up at the cash register, Susan checking out one of the ladies with the art books. He also sees the box of books he was in the middle of shelving. A task he won't be able to complete. He figures Hector will do it.

*These goddamn kids and their enthusiasm. Afraid to break the rules. Afraid to put their necks on the line for what they believe in. I'd rather live on my feet than die on my knees.*

Randy looks down and realizes he can almost see his knees through his worn jeans.

He turns and leaves Bookstorage through the back door, slowly walking to where his car is straddling two spaces. The parking lot's quiet; there aren't many cars around. He can hear the hum of the freeway on the other side of the building.

When he gets to his Tercel, he sees a piece of paper stuck under one of his windshield wipers. Written in block letters with red marker, the note says ASSHOLE.

# 3: NEARLY LOST YOU

There's a car in front of the practice space. Mark wonders if it belongs to Steve or Gary or some other guy who's in some other band who's here to practice early on a Saturday. The car, a beat up old Chrysler with an I ♥ ZOMBIES bumper sticker, is parked underneath a faded sign that says THE JAM ROOM. Below this sits a musical staff with assorted notes. Squinting through the windshield, the notes look to Mark like G, F#, G, A, D, A, G, F#. He whistles the tune, but doesn't recognize it.

Mark parks, turns off the engine, and just sits there. It's what he used to do when the band first got together. Whenever Mark showed up to practice—if only Gary's car was there—he'd sit until Steve showed up. He didn't want to go in and talk to Gary because he didn't know him. Steve had known Gary since they were kids, but Mark only knew Steve from mutual friends, and really didn't know Gary at all. So Mark would stall until Steve showed up, and then act like he just got there, too.

Mark sighs and gets out of the car. He grabs his guitar from the trunk, as well as a small suitcase that holds a few pedals, cords, spare strings, and a strap.

The one-story building is red brick with wooden slats painted blue where windows used to be. The front door is open and the lobby—a small vestibule with an iMac on a desk, two old wingback chairs covered in stains, and a water cooler—is empty. The walls are decorated with records he's never heard of by bands he doesn't know. To the right, next to the men's room, he sees STUDIO A. As he approaches, muffled sounds come from behind the doors. Someone's tuning up.

Mark opens the double doors. The first thing he sees is a drum set sitting along the large far wall, sandwiched between a huge rectangular bass amp and a squat Fender amp with a silver face. In the corner are various musical odds and ends—microphone stands, keyboards, amps, amp heads, and drums. While Mark stands there waiting someone comes out from behind the bass amp. It's Gary. He's wearing skinny green jeans, a tight black shirt with a red-and-blue bull's-eye, and a pair of Converse sneakers held together with duct tape. His hair has thinned and is too black to be natural. Bangs hang into his eyes and, when he smiles, Mark can see brown, stained teeth.

"It's funny."

Hearing Gary's voice again sends chills down Mark's spine. He hasn't heard him speak for two decades. The voice is exactly like he remembers.

"What?"

"For so many years," Gary says, "I had this big long speech of what I was going to say if I ever saw you again. For a while there, I wasn't sure I ever would. See you again, I mean. But I always wanted to be prepared, just in case."

"Yeah?"

*Maybe this was a bad idea. I wish Steve were here. I should have waited outside.*

"I used to rehearse it," Gary says. "Over and over. I'd even revise it from time to time. Make it longer, shorter, whatever. But then that went away and I—I just had questions. About why you did what you did. Why you walked out. I just wanted answers. And then, finally, that went away, too. And now . . ."

"And now, what?"

"Now, it's just good to see you."

Gary sticks out his hand and Mark shakes it.

"You too."

Mark lets go first.

"So, have you been back before now?" Gary says. "To Kitty, I mean. I never really heard anything."

"No." Mark looks at the ground. He kicks at one of the legs of a microphone stand. "This is my first time since we left back in '93."

"Must be strange."

Mark grins.

"That's one word for it."

From behind them there's noise. Gary and Mark turn.

"Sorry I'm late."

Steve enters the room carrying a pair of drumsticks in one hand and a bottle of water in the other. He's wearing blue sweatpants and a navy blue sweatshirt that says GO CAVALIERS in orange letters. A paunch pushes out the sweatshirt, showing pink skin.

"Oh, my god," Steve says. "Mark? Holy *shit*. Come here, man."

Steve rushes Mark and envelopes him in a hug.

"Hey, Steve. Good to see you."

They separate and Steve nods to Gary.

"Gary, my man, good to see you. It's been a while."

"Don't you guys hang out?" Mark says.

"Not like we used to," Gary says. "Not like the old days."

"But we have recently."

After Steve says this, Gary shoots him a look.

"Anyway, we're back together," Steve says. "Bottlecap. I never would have thought."

"Guys," Gary says. "I hate to break up this warm and fuzzy moment, but we're not Bottlecap until we play some music. Right now we're just three middle-aged dudes standing around. What do you say we plug in and get started?"

Mark and Steve nod. Gary grabs his battered Fender Jazz bass from a stand and straps it on. Steve moves behind the drums. As Mark gets his Mustang out of its case, he says to Steve, "Do you still play much?"

"In the garage. When I have time." He does a few fills and rolls. The sound ricochets throughout the room. Mark's ears already hurt.

"But at home all I have are electronic drums. I play with head-phones on."

Mark turns on the amp and plugs in his guitar. A huge electric crackle, as loud as thunder, fills the room. He's been practicing the songs back in his apartment on an acoustic guitar. He hasn't played his electric—through an amp—in a long time.

Mark tunes up, plays a few notes, then moves on to chords. Across the room, Gary's fiddling with his bass.

"Sorry, guys. This thing won't stay in tune. Give me another minute."

Mark turns to Steve.

"So, you sell cars now?"

Steve blushes.

"It's my brother's dealership. Do you remember him?"

Mark thinks.

"Phil, right?"

"That's him."

"He was a good guy. Played in bands, too."

"Yeah, but he stopped a long time ago. He bought the dealership from a guy when it was going under and turned it around. He offered me a part-time job about ten years ago, and I've been there ever since. I'm now senior salesman. It's a nice gig." Steve finally looks up from his drums. "You got a car?"

"In Manhattan? No. But if I ever need one, I'll make sure I come see you."

"I bet the publicity's been good for you," Gary says, still tuning up. The notes rattle the wires underneath the snare drum. "I saw the dealership mentioned in the paper."

Steve blushes again. Mark doesn't remember him blushing this much.

"It doesn't hurt, I admit. Maybe it'll mean a spike at the end of the month. It's always tough to meet sales goals."

Mark nods and then goes back to warming up. Steve plays various beats, pausing to rearrange the placement of the drums—moving the snare in closer, making the crash a little higher. Gary finishes tuning up and turns to Steve and Mark.

"All set," Gary says. "I've got all our songs on my iPod in case we need to remember any of the parts. Otherwise, let's start with a slow one and work our way up to the faster stuff. Sound good?"

Mark and Steve both nod.

"Okay, then," Gary says. "'Parisian Broke'?"

Mark and Steve nod again. Then there's just silence.

"Steve," Gary says. "Count us off. Remember?"

"Oh, right. Sorry."

Steve raises his drumsticks, hits them together and says, not much above a whisper, "One-two-three-four."

The parking lot's full of minivans, station wagons, SUVs. No sports cars, no convertibles. Ashley can't see a motorcycle anywhere. As she gets out of her car and walks towards the entrance to Babies R Us, she peeks into various vehicles and sees car seats, toys, bottles. Crumbs litter every surface and, in every car, there are Cheerios. So many Cheerios. She holds her breath as she approaches the double doors.

*I can do this.*

Ashley walks through the store, aisles on either side stretching out into different sections—diapers, bath stuff, cribs, slides for the back-yard. Her plan had been to run in and grab the first thing she saw, but since it's barely eleven she has time before meeting Craig at noon.

She's wearing a black skirt, burgundy sweater set, and black high heels. As she walks, her shoes click loudly against the shiny floors. The noise can be heard even above the children's music they're piping in from the ceiling speakers. No one else is wearing heels. Or a skirt. Or makeup. Ashley looks like the "before" picture and everyone else looks like the "after."

While the parents with kids all look exhausted, the pregnant women all look smug. They walk with one hand on their bellies, as if already holding their precious babies. Ashley stares at one woman for an uncomfortably long time, trying to see movement—to see the baby kick—but the woman gets spooked and leaves the aisle, disappearing to find her husband.

As she makes her way through the store—feeling stared at by all of those babies' faces on the packages—Ashley can't help but think of Charlottesville. It's been so long, and she's blocked so much of it out of her mind, that the only things that come back to her are vague images and sensations.

Getting lost on the way to the clinic.

The lobby.

The receptionist who wouldn't look her in the eye.

A metal tray.

That sucking sound.

Tears, pain, and almost instant regret.

She remembers how, as she lay in the recovery room, she realized her relationship with Craig was over. Even though they'd made the decision together, Ashley knew she'd always hold it against him. There could be no future if she was always going to be angry about the past. After they stayed the night in Charlottesville—it was Craig's idea to not do the procedure close to home, in an attempt to spare her pain and memories—they returned to Kitty and tried to act like nothing had happened. Tried to go back to the way their lives used to be. But after a few weeks, Ashley asked Craig to move out.

Ashley stayed until the lease ran out, and then got her own place on the other side of town. She dated for a couple of years, a few nice guys here and there, but none of them turned into anything serious. She ran into Andrew shortly after her thirty-fifth birthday. She hadn't seen him since the nineties, since she'd been with Craig. Andrew assumed they were still together. "Where's Craig?" is the first thing Andrew said when he spotted her in line for the bathroom at a party being thrown by a mutual acquaintance. Ashley just laughed, threw back her head, and said, "How should I know?" They began dating that week.

After that, they had a few nice years. They had a fun honeymoon. Every few years they took a vacation. They both liked their jobs. Life seemed ahead of them, and they were excited to be facing it together. They spooned each other in the morning, kissed each other good night, and said "I love you" at the end of phone calls, and meant it.

Early on in the relationship, they both agreed they didn't want kids. By then, all of their friends had kids. One kid, two kids, and sometimes—though Ashley couldn't figure out why—a third. But when Ashley was about to turn forty, she began to feel different. She broached the subject with Andrew, and found that he was having the same thoughts. She was overjoyed. They hugged and kissed and began planning the future, suggesting names and figuring out which room in the house would be the nursery.

On Ashley's forty-first birthday, they tried to get pregnant. At first all this entailed was going off the pill and making appointments to have sex. Nothing happened. She then began buying ovulation kits and keeping track of her cycles with NASA-like precision. This went on for a few years, always with the same results. By the time she and Andrew finally decided to go to a fertility specialist, they were told it was too late for any affordable options. Ashley broke down when she received the news.

After that, she drifted away from her friends who were parents. Ashley couldn't stand to hear about children, nor continue to fake a smile as they showed her photos of grinning or sleeping babies on their iPhones. This meant withdrawing from pretty much everyone she knew, but she felt she had to do it. She even started avoiding her parents because all they wanted to know was when she and Andrew were going to give them grandchildren. She hated that that's all they wanted from her. She hated even more that her only response to the question was "never."

Now, wandering aisle after aisle at Babies R Us—she sees all the tired but happy couples shuffling with their overstuffed diaper bags and carts loaded with toys—she can't believe how dumb she'd been. She and her stupid friends. Taking the pill, using condoms, doing everything they could to avoid having kids, then waking up one day and wanting the opposite. It was like something out of *1984*.

Six months ago Ashley saw a young disabled girl at the mall. Down syndrome. Ashley cried. She wept. She hated the thoughts she had. *I'll even take that. Just to say I was a parent. Just to watch someone grow up. I don't mind. God,*—she never talked to God, didn't believe in God, had grown to hate God—*just give me something. Anything. To love.* But even that didn't happen.

"Will this be all for you?"

Ashley looks up, startled.

She's in the checkout line. She doesn't remember picking an item, or approaching a cashier, but here she is.

The people who shop at Babies R Us might be parents or soon-to-be-parents, but the people who work there are kids. First jobs for awkward teenagers. This girl, BRITTANY according to her nametag, has flawless skin and a wonderful smile. Teeth as white as the paint job of a brand-new car.

Somehow Ashley manages to pull out and hand over her credit card. The young girl, somewhat spooked—her bright eyes now not-so-bright—looks down, embarrassed. She quickly scans the three-pack of onesies and slides Ashley's credit card through the machine. Ashley signs with an *X*, ripping the paper as she does so. She grabs the bag and walks out of the store.

She gets into her Prius, throws the Babies R Us bag into the back-seat, grabs her purse and fishes around for her bottle of Protraxanon. When she finds it, it makes a noise just like the rattles she saw back in the store. She swallows a pill dry.

Ashley drives across town in a daze.

Walking up to the restaurant, from the sidewalk, she sees Craig sitting at a table near the window. She thought he would be sitting in the back, in a booth half-hidden in shadows. Ashley takes a deep breath and enters the restaurant.

Nolan's is crowded, most of the tables filled. Conversation drowns out the music playing in the background. A hostess approaches carrying a stack of menus. She has a spring in her step and her light-brown hair is pulled back into a ponytail that moves behind her like a windshield wiper when she walks. Ashley usually wants to kill young, pretty girls like this. But right now, her mind is too clouded to be jealous.

"Hi there, welcome to Nolan's. How can I help you?"

Craig had emailed to let her know he'd made a reservation, but Ashley can't bear to say his name. So instead she says, "I'm just meeting a friend. I think he's here already."

The hostess steps aside to let her by.

As Ashley walks through the dining room, she tries to surreptitiously glance at the crowd to see if there's anyone she recognizes, friends of hers, people who know her—anyone who might later tell Andrew they saw her here with Craig.

As she approaches him from behind, Ashley can see how much hair he's lost. He has a bald spot on the top of his head and—on the sides and the back—the hair is thin and wispy, like cotton candy. His scalp is red and freckled.

The skin on his neck, leading into a pressed blue Oxford shirt, is freckled and flaky. That body used to lie next to her, do things to her, but it means nothing to her now. She sees a book on the table. A Faulkner paperback that looks vaguely familiar.

Craig senses her presence and rises, turning toward her. They lock eyes. Neither of them speaks. A busboy comes by and clears the plates from the table next to theirs. Finally, Craig smiles and speaks.

"Hi."

He reaches out his hand; Ashley awkwardly takes it.

"Hi."

Craig's hand is clammy, his grip loose.

She can't believe how old he looks. His teeth are yellow, his hair's mostly gone, and his chin sags into his open shirt. She looks for the younger version of him in the face he has now—pudgy, reddened, spots on his nose—but it's gone. That Craig no longer exists. Two words enter her head that never really have before.

*Middle age.*

Craig says, "Can you believe this?"

After he says this, he grins. Ashley discovers there's still some charm in his smile. It reminds her of why she fell for him in the first place.

"No, I can't."

"Yes, you can."

Steve leans forward on the drums. He's sweating profusely and breathing heavily, his bulging belly disappears and returns with each breath.

"Seriously, Gary. I can't go on."

They've been playing all morning, and it's finally starting to sound good. They're playing "Parisian Broke" and "Bad Skin Day" pretty well, and "Birthday Ache" is coming along nicely. One or two more tries and they'll all know their parts. Another hour and they'll sound like a band again.

"Seriously." Steve, out of breath, pauses before saying more. "Let's . . . take a break."

"Fine," Gary says. "But a quick one."

Mark pulls out his phone. "Jesus, it's noon. Why don't we go out and get a bite?"

"I . . . I," Steve says, still breathing heavily. "I brought . . . a little something . . . for us."

Gary and Mark glance at each other before turning to Steve.

"You packed a lunch?"

"My wife made it . . . for all of us. It's just some sandwiches . . . and chips. Coleslaw." He gets up from behind the drums, still panting. His sweatshirt is soaked through. "Fruit salad . . . and cheese. Be right back."

As Steve leaves the room, Gary and Mark put down their guitars. Steve returns a minute later with a wicker basket and sets it down. He opens it up and pulls out plastic plates, handing one to Mark and another to Gary.

"Wow," Mark says. "She's a regular Martha Stewart."

Steve unpacks the rest of the food, placing everything on top of Mark's amp.

Gary, chewing, says, "You should see her, Mark. Spokesmodel category all the way. But nice. Smart, too. Steve, what was she before you knocked her up?"

Mark says, "You have kids?"

"Yeah, three. Two girls and a boy. Eight, six, and four." Steve turns to Gary. "She was a lawyer and will be again someday, once the kids are a little older."

"Jesus. Three kids."

"What?" Gary says. "You thought he drove a minivan to carry around his electronic drums?"

As he eats his lunch, Mark begins to feel clammy as the sweat turns cool on his skin.

"How about you?" Steve says.

"Me?" Mark says. "No kids." He takes a big bite of his sandwich, hoping the question will blow over.

"Married?"

"No."

"Dating anyone?"

"No."

To get the spotlight off of him, Mark turns to Gary. "So, you still play in bands?"

"Three," Gary says proudly. "One's kind of a home recording project, but the other two play shows."

"Steve, they any good?"

"What are you asking *him* for? You think he gets out anymore?"

"Gary's right." Steve picks raspberries out of a Tupperware container with a plastic fork. "With the kids and the dealership, it doesn't leave time for much else."

Mark tries to remember Steve all those years ago. He acted like such a punk when they got the deal and went to LA. It's not that Mark thought Steve would never grow up; it's that he never thought he'd have to.

"I'll give you my latest cassette," Gary says.

"Cassette?" Mark says.

"Guys, I'm telling you, cassettes are making a comeback." Gary takes a swig from a bottle of water on the floor and then checks his silver combination watch and digital calculator. "Speaking of which, so are we. Let's get back to work."

His mouth full of food, Steve says, "I'm still eating."

"Swallow," Gary says. "Chewing is optional. Let's *go*."

Craig motions to the chair with its back to the window. As she sits down, he notices she's wearing a skirt and heels. He's glad he wore the blazer. He sits down after she does.

Ashley reaches for the book and picks it up. It's *A Fable* by William Faulkner. It's how they met.

"It's my original copy. Do you remember?"

She turns it over and over in her hands. The cover is worn, the pages—many of them dog-eared—are yellow.

"Yes. I was looking at a copy in the college bookstore when you approached me. You said something about 'Count No Count' and I was impressed. I shouldn't have been. I thought you liked Faulkner. Looking back on it now, you were just hitting on me."

He grins.

"Do you blame me?"

"I do, in a way."

Craig's face falls.

"I mean, I wish I'd known that at the time," she says. "When you invited me for coffee to talk about the book, I thought you actually wanted to talk about the book."

A waiter appears, introduces himself, and offers to get each of them a drink. He's young and good-looking and Craig instantly hates him. He lets Ashley order first and is glad she asks for a glass of wine. He orders one, too. For a moment he considers suggesting they get a bottle, but doesn't want to push his luck. When the waiter leaves, Ashley puts down the book and picks up the menu.

While she's trying to decide what to order, Craig pretends he's looking at his menu but really he's looking at Ashley. She's heavier than he remembers and has wrinkles at the corners of her mouth. Craig can tell that the excessive makeup around her eyes is less to accentuate them than it is to cover up dark circles underneath them.

He tries to remember life with Ashley—sleeping with her, kissing her, even just talking to her. Almost nothing comes back. He has vague sensations and memories, but after all this time they're just fuzzy snapshots. He can barely reconcile those memories with the person sitting in front of him now. This could be a business lunch. He could be meeting her for the first time.

As Ashley puts down her menu, Craig notices the rings. Something inside of him deflates.

"You're married."

For a second, Ashley seems embarrassed.

"Oh, *this*." Her thumb begins turning her wedding band around and around. The engagement ring, vintage-looking with a big diamond surrounded by smaller ones, stays in place.

"How long?"

"Going on eight years."

"Wow." He knows he should leave it there. It is, after all, all the information he needs. She's married. She found someone else. Any additional bit of information is just a needle that's going to cause him pain. But he has to ask. "To whom?"

Before she can answer the waiter returns with their wine. Ashley orders pasta and Craig, panicking, orders a steak salad even though that's not what he wants. As the waiter's walking away, Craig means to call him back, to change his order. His mouth opens but no sound comes out. He turns back to Ashley.

"To whom?" Craig repeats.

"What?"

"Your ring. You said you're married. I asked, 'to *whom*.'"

A few seconds go by before she answers. Finally, she speaks. When she does, it's barely above a whisper.

"Andrew."

"*Andrew*? From twenty years ago, Andrew?"

"Yes, Craig. Yes."

"Why, that fucking little rat. I *knew* he was into you. But you always swore—"

"Stop. I just—don't. Just, stop."

When neither of them speaks, the background noise of the restaurant fills the space between them. Craig clenches his fist, his palms feeling hot and moist. He wants to ask whether she was seeing him while they were going out, or how soon after they broke up did she and Andrew get together. But he figures none of that matters now. He pushes all of those thoughts aside and, when he does, the only thing that's left is the regret that he let her go.

"What about you?"

"Me?" Craig says. "What do you mean?"

Ashley smiles.

"Married, silly. You're not wearing a ring."

Even though Craig knows that he's not, he raises his left hand and looks. Even though he didn't wear it for long—just a couple years—every now and then he can still feel it, the way amputees can still feel limbs they've lost. The same goes for Gemma herself. Some nights, in bed, he could swear that she's still there.

"No," Craig says. "But I was."

"For how long? To whom?"

"It was years ago. It didn't last, obviously. Her name was Gemma."

"What happened?"

Craig stares out into the parking lot, thinking for a few seconds. He watches as the Range Rover he parked next to pulls out of the parking lot.

"We wanted different things, I guess." He stops for a second to take a sip of his wine. "We weren't happy, and I couldn't make her happy. We finally decided we might as well end it while we were somewhat young."

"Where is she now?"

"DC. She moved there to get into politics. I never really asked which side."

Ashley reaches for her wine and, when she does, the sunlight hits the diamond in her engagement ring, causing it to shine.

"Do you have any kids?"

"No," Craig says. "We never—that is, Gemma didn't—"

A busboy comes by to refill their water glasses. When he approaches, Craig stops speaking. He takes another sip of wine. The busboy leaves.

"How about you and Andrew?"

Ashley answers with a small shake of her head, no.

The waiter returns and wordlessly places Ashley's plate of pasta in front of her. As he puts down Craig's salad, he says, "Here you are, sir." But Craig's too depressed to feel old.

As he pokes at his salad, Craig wonders whether Ashley's happy. He thinks about Andrew. He wonders what he's like after all these years. Craig didn't like him much back then, so he doubts he'd like him much now.

*Pompous little prick. Always talking about obscure books and foreign movies. Who was he trying to impress?*

The Faulkner novel catches Craig's eye. He quickly picks it up and puts it on the floor.

"So," Ashley says. "What are you up to these days?"

"I work at one of the new startups downtown. It's called Seatr."

"Cedar? Like the tree?"

"No, Seat-er. S-E-A-T-R."

Craig finishes his wine and flags down the waiter for another glass.

The waiter asks if Ashley will have another, but she just shakes her head.

"Crimes against grammar aside," Ashley says, "what does the site actually do?"

"We sell plane tickets. Or, actually, we resell them. When people can't use them."

"How does that work, exactly?"

"Let's say you bought a ticket to go from Los Angeles to New York next week, but something's come up and you can't make it. The ticket's nonrefundable and to change it to a later date would cost a few hundred bucks. What do you?"

Ashley considers this.

"I don't know. Forfeit the ticket, I guess. Lose the money."

Craig grins.

"Not anymore. Go onto Seatr and list the ticket for sale. You set the price, and we'll match you up with someone who wants to buy your ticket. We send whoever bought the ticket the confirmation code, and we send you the money. After, of course, we take a cut."

"Let me get this straight. You're *scalping* airline tickets?"

"We provide a valuable service for people who have a need and for other people who want to pay for that—need."

The waiter delivers his wine and Craig takes a sip.

Ashley says, "But is that even legal? Like, what happens when some guy gets to the airport and has my ticket? I can't image the airlines would ever—"

"Beta," Craig interrupts. "We're in *beta*."

They both cross their legs, accidentally brushing against each other under the table. This sends a shock through Craig. He looks for recognition on Ashley's face—that they've touched after all these years—but there's nothing.

He says, "What happened to us?"

Behind him there's the noise of the restaurant, more intense than before now that people are finishing their lunch and leaving. Craig can hear the same cheery hostess at the front telling everyone to have a good day.

"You *know* what happened to us," Ashley says. "You had big ideas, all these dreams. You were going to conquer the world and, when it looked like it wasn't going to happen, you blamed me."

"Ash, that's not fair."

"Don't call me Ash—"

"Ash, please."

"Fine, then it just didn't work out, that's all. And why are you putting me on the spot like this? It was mutual."

"It wasn't mutual. You asked me to leave."

Craig figures there's no reason to pursue this, so he stops. He had only asked because he thought it'd invoke fond memories. Maybe even some longing for the old days, when they were young and belonged to each other. He hoped Ashley would give a wry smile and Craig could pretend that she was the one that got away. Instead, it just led to the old anger.

Changing the subject, Craig says, "Tell me about your job."

"God," Ashley says. "I don't want to talk about that."

"Okay. Then where do you guys live?"

She tells Craig about their house, all the crap in their garage, and Andrew. How he's teaching and working on a novel. Craig listens, nodding his head, trying to see if the woman talking to him across the table is somehow still the girl he fell in love with all of those years ago.

After another half hour of small talk, the check comes.

"Let me get this," Craig says.

Ashley doesn't protest.

As he's dropping some cash on the table, Ashley picks up her purse from the ground and pulls out an iPhone. Craig wonders if she's texting Andrew and, if so, what? Surely she's going to lie about lunch. He grabs the Faulkner from the floor and sticks it into one of the pockets of his blazer.

Ashley stands and Craig follows her through Nolan's. Outside, it's even hotter than before. Craig walks next to Ashley as she heads to a corner of the parking lot. He's tempted to try and hold her hand, but doesn't have the nerve. She finally stops and pulls out a set of car keys from her purse.

She turns to face him.

"Thanks, Craig. Despite everything, it was good to see you."

"Could we—do it again sometime?"

"We'll see."

Ashley leans in and gives him a hug. Looking down at the top of her head, Craig can tell that she dyes her hair. He tries to stretch out the hug, to have it turn into something else—his arms begin to move down her back—but she pulls away.

Craig watches as she gets into the car, starts it, and slowly exits the parking lot.

Gary stops the song halfway through by taking his hands off his bass and waving them in the air. Mark stops first, glad to have the break. Steve, his head down and in his own world, takes a few more seconds before he notices he's the only one playing. When he finally stops, the drums continue echoing throughout the room.

"Steve, dude," Gary says. "You're coming out of the choruses *way* too fast. Slow down, okay? Take it down a notch. Seriously."

Steve nods while breathing heavily. He took his sweatshirt off hours ago and is now wearing a white Haverkamp Motors T-shirt, soaked with sweat.

"And Mark, you're slowing down a bit. Are you getting tired?"

Mark wipes sweat from his forehead with his sleeve.

"I'm fine. It's just been a while since I played for this long."

"Maybe we should take another break," Steve says.

"Fine." Gary walks over to where a blue Dickies jacket hangs on a microphone stand. He fishes around in the various pockets and pulls out a pack of Marlboros. He lights a cigarette with a Zippo lighter.

"You still smoke?" Mark says.

"Yeah, why?" Gary exhales a cloud of smoke. "You?"

"Quit years ago."

"Fucking Boy Scout."

"Guys." Steve looks at his watch. "It's getting late. I should be heading home."

"Late?" Gary glances at his wrist. "It's four."

"I'm thirsty," Mark says. "Maybe I'll run out and get a few bottles of water."

"Shut up, the both of you." Gary points at each of them with his cigarette. "We're going to practice for a few more hours and then we're going to get a pizza and eat it here. We'll get some beer, too. That way we can practice after we eat. But we're not going anywhere."

"Come on," Steve says. "It's sounding good."

"It's sounding *okay*." Gary tunes up his bass, the cigarette dangling from his lips. "But we have a lot more work to do before next week, so let's all put in a full day, if you don't mind."

"Oh, I don't mind. It's Robin who's going to mind." Steve pulls out his phone and begins writing a text. "And by the way, put out that cigarette. You're edgy, we get it."

Gary laughs as he drops the cigarette into a coffee cup. It goes out with a fizzle.

"Before I forget, guys, Dave texted me earlier."

"Yeah?" Mark sits down on his amp. The tips of his fingers are numb and his back hasn't hurt this much in years. When he swallows, his throat feels like sandpaper. "What'd he have to say?"

"A guy from DISContent got in touch and wants us to do an in-store this week a couple of days before the show."

"That old record store's still around?" Mark says. "I would have thought it went out of business a long time ago."

"Dave thinks he can get some local media to cover it if we play. Maybe a TV crew or something like that. Would be good publicity for the show."

Steve says, "When does he want us to do it?"

"Well, it'd just be Mark and me. They want us to do a few songs 'unplugged.' Acoustic."

"There's also that story the guy's writing for the *Times-Dispatch*," Mark says. "Won't that be *enough* publicity?"

"Come on, Mark," Gary says. "The songs sound great on an acoustic. Remember when you used to give us cassettes of demos? I still have all of those, and they sound great."

Back when they first became a band, Mark wrote all the songs on an acoustic guitar, most of them in that apartment he revisited the other day. Whenever he finished a new song, he'd record a simple version of it—just his guitar and his voice—onto his four track. Then he'd make cassettes of the new songs for Gary and Steve so they could work out their parts ahead of their practices.

"Let me think about it."

"Yeah, well, don't think too long. I'm sure they'll want an answer like yesterday so they can do some advertising and get the word out on social media."

"Look at you," Mark says. "Mr. Professional."

Gary grins.

"This isn't my first rodeo."

"No," Mark says, "at your first rodeo you fell off and the bull kicked you in the head."

"At least *I* got back up and tried again."

Mark's about to respond when Steve says, "Guys, let's stay focused, okay?"

Gary and Mark nod.

"Okay," Gary says. "Let's keep going. From the top."

Steve wipes the sweat from his forehead, counts off, and they start again.

Grace comes down the stairs carrying a hamper filled with clothes. Charles is on the couch doing two things Grace doesn't like him to do: working on the weekend and sitting on the couch in dirty clothes. He mowed the lawn earlier. She can smell the cut grass from across the room.

"Now, *sweetheart.*" She gets to the bottom step and places the hamper on the floor. "This is *our* time. You promised me you weren't going to bring work home on the weekends anymore, remember?"

"Did I?" Charles runs a hand over his head. He has practically no hair left so he keeps it short, just a few centimeters or so where it still grows around his ears and above his neckline. As he rubs, he feels the oily slickness of sunscreen. To prevent skin cancer, his doctor advised him to put on sunscreen whenever he went outside. It was yet another indignity foisted on him by the loss of his hair.

"Yes, you naughty boy. You *did.*"

Grace joins him on the couch.

"Sorry. It's just I—there are a few things I need to get to before Monday." This is a lie. He's just doing busywork and waiting to receive word from Tom about his talk with O'Brien, to see if Dylan's promotion can be stopped. "Maddie still in the backyard?"

"She and Zoe and Ellis are playing princess."

"Are they taking turns, or are they all princesses?"

"They all are, of course. Speaking of which, I invited the Nearys over for dinner."

Ellis is Roy and Ronnie's daughter.

"When?"

"Next Saturday."

"Just them?" Charles says. "Because I also kind of invited the Hendersons to a barbeque."

"When did you do that, silly?"

"The other day. I asked John while we were taking in the recycling bins. Are they bringing the kids?"

"That's odd. Elaine just texted and she didn't say anything about it. No, not the kids. They're getting a sitter."

Charles read an article recently about how most people couldn't tell you the names of their neighbors. It said that people live in isolation, and not just in the big cities. Even in the suburbs, supposedly, people keep to themselves. That's not the case in Tiger Bay. That's not the case for Charles. He can tell you the names of pretty much everyone on his street. He runs into them constantly. Working in the yard, taking out the trash, or out for walks with Maddie. They're not just neighbors; they're friends. In the summers there are barbecues, play dates, game nights. Inflatable pools are set up on front lawns and families just drift from house to house chatting while the kids leap from pool to pool with never time to get dry, the toddler version of that Cheever story.

"Well, maybe they're waiting for a better offer," Charles says. "Or maybe they already have an offer out to someone else, so Elaine doesn't want to commit to us."

"Do you think it's that new couple down the block? The one with the twins? Elaine let it slip that they'd been over there for brunch."

"Brunch whores."

"You're the worst." She slaps him playfully. "But I guess we can push John and Elaine to Sunday."

Charles stops typing for a second as Maddie and the girls erupt into laughter in the backyard. There's not a sound he loves more than that laugh.

"You looking forward to seeing Randy tonight?"

Charles smiles. "Yeah, actually. But it's weird."

"What's weird about it?"

"We had a lot of fun, and we were good friends, but that was a long time ago. I've changed a lot since then."

He looks around the house.

"What is it?" Grace says.

"I don't know. I don't want him to think I sold out."

"Why, because you live in a house?"

"Because we live in Tiger Bay. And we have nice cars. And a daughter in private school."

She says, sarcastically, "You should be ashamed of yourself."

"You don't understand. We used to make fun of the people who lived around here. Who lived in these big houses and worried about their lawns and their careers. And now that's me. I guess it just goes to show—"

But he stops talking.

"What, darling?"

"I don't know." He hears Maddie again in the backyard. He smiles. "It's just funny. It looked bad then. It doesn't look so bad now."

"Well, *however* it looks, I need to finish the laundry and get started on dinner. And you need take a shower. I'll feed Maddie early and she can watch TV upstairs while we're eating. Okay?"

"That's great, sweetheart. Thanks."

Charles leans in to kiss her but Grace smiles and pulls back.

"Shower, sweetie. Shower."

Charles gets up and climbs the stairs. After a quick shower he comes downstairs and does more work in his office. Down the hall he can hear Grace cooking and Maddie eating. As she has her dinner, Maddie tells Grace all about how Zoe, Ellis, and she played in the backyard. Even though it's the same routine they always follow— Grace has heard this recap a million times—she listens attentively and asks questions she already knows the answers to.

Charles looks at the clock and sees that it's almost seven. He calls down the hall.

"Get ready, guys. He's almost here."

"Who, Daddy?"

Grace answers.

"Daddy's old friend, Randy. From back when daddy had hair."

Grace and Maddie both laugh. Charles turns back to his laptop. As he's going through emails from last week, a new one pops up. It's from Tom.

*Finally.*

Charles sits up in his chair, nervous to open it. He looks and makes sure that Grace and Maddie are still in the kitchen. He hears water running—Grace probably doing the dishes—while Maddie's singing "Call Me Maybe." He opens the email.

*Charles,*

*Sorry to bother you over the weekend, but I just had a preliminary discussion with O'Brien about what you and I discussed the other day and, while he was initially taken aback, he eventually agreed about our assessment of the situation. He even confided in me that he's had similar suspicions. Per our discussion, I now need some documentation. Once I have some proof, we can move forward. Let's try and meet by Wednesday. Get me something before then. And, of course, this is all in strictest confidence.*

*—Tom*

*PS: Don't bullshit me for a second that you don't want that job.*

By the time Charles finishes reading the email, his heart's beating fast and he feels flushed. He puts his hand to his forehead and discovers it's hot. Sweat begins to form on his upper lip.

*Documentation. Proof. Wednesday.*

The doorbell rings and Charles jumps. Looking up, he sees it's ten past seven.

Grace calls out.

"Charles, you want to get that?"

Charles closes his laptop, exhales, and walks into the hallway. As he approaches the door, he can see the top of Randy's head through three rectangular panes of glass. Charles is jealous that Randy still has hair.

He opens the door and can't believe that Randy's standing there. For a second Charles flashes back to high school, to that first day in science class their sophomore year. Randy doesn't look much different.

"Dude," he says.

"Randy, my God. This is amazing. Come in, come in."

When Charles puts his hand out for Randy to shake, he sees that Randy's nails are long and dirty, each one tipped with a crescent of black.

"Thanks."

As Charles steps aside to let Randy enter the house, he smells cigarette smoke and the faint aroma of pot. Closing the door, Charles frowns at Randy's battered Tercel parked at the curb. Grace and Maddie enter the hallway from the kitchen.

"Guys, *this* is Randy. Randy, this is my wife, Grace."

"Hey," Randy says.

"Hey," Grace says.

"And who's this?" When Randy bends over to make eye contact with Maddie, he burps. She steps back, behind Grace.

"That's our daughter, Maddie."

"Hey," Maddie says.

"Hey," Randy says.

There's an awkward silence for a second. No one knows who has the next move. Charles finally says, "So, Randy, want a drink?"

"You bet I do."

Without waiting and without really knowing where he's going, Randy walks past Charles and enters the den.

"Power lines."

"What?"

"Power lines," Mark repeats. "You asked me what the strangest thing about being back in Kitty is."

Steve stuffs another slice of pizza into his mouth. Gary's sitting cross-legged on the floor while Mark sits on the edge of the bass drum.

The tuning pegs are digging into his ass. Steve's on his drumming throne, the box of pizza open on the snare drum. There are four slices left. The plastic rings from a six-pack of beer hang from the crash cymbal, while the rings from another six-pack sit on the ground, three cans already empty and crumpled while the other three are currently being swigged by Mark, Gary, and Steve.

"I just can't get over how many power lines there are in this town. When you drive down the road, that's all you see. Power lines."

Chewing, Steve says, "I guess I never noticed it."

Gary laughs and looks around the room.

"Jesus fucking Christ, guys."

"What?"

"I can't believe that we're sitting here talking about goddamn power lines when the show's barely a week away."

"You asked how I was doing," Mark says. "What it was like being back in Kitty. I'm telling you."

"About power lines?"

"It's just something I've noticed."

Gary finishes his beer, crushes it in his hand, and throws it across the room.

"Guys, we need to talk about the show."

Steve goes in for another slice.

"What about it?"

"Well," Gary says. "I know a guy who can make us some T-shirts."

"You mean Bottlecap shirts?" Mark says.

Gary points at Steve.

"No, I mean Haverkamp Motors shirts. *Yes*, Bottlecap shirts. Dave told me he's going to be selling the last of the Violent Revolution stock at the show. Our early singles and shit like that. He mentioned the Deer Park still has a bunch of T-shirts and he's going to unload them. So I thought it'd be fun if we had T-shirts, too."

"The Deer Park? Figures." Steve laughs. "Those guys could barely get arrested in this town, let alone anywhere else. No wonder they still have that crap."

"But what would the shirts say?" Mark says. "I don't have time to design anything. I didn't even bring my computer."

Gary grins.

"It's all taken care of."

"What?" Steve says. "What's taken care of?"

"The shirts."

"But how?"

Gary says, "I have a few tricks up my sleeve."

Mark takes a swig of beer and then twists around to grab another slice of pizza. Chewing, he looks at Gary.

*What's he up to?*

As Charles walks to where a bar's set up in the corner of the den—bottles of liquor stand next to an array of glasses and an ice bucket with a pair of tongs attached to the side—Randy gets a whiff of his old friend. Charles smells like Polo and lawn clippings.

"So, what are we drinking?"

"Whiskey," Charles says. "Little ice?"

"Hit me."

Behind them, Randy hears Grace tell Maddie to go upstairs to watch TV. Charles goes to work on the drinks, ice cubes clinking into the glasses.

"Dude, your wife is hot."

"Uh, thanks, Randy. How about you?"

Charles hands Randy his drink. Randy takes a huge sip, drinking almost half of it in one gulp. Charles takes a small sip and sits down on a wooden chair.

"How about me, what?"

"You seeing someone?"

Randy just shakes his head.

"Relationships haven't really worked for me for the past couple of—decades."

Grace calls out from the kitchen.

"Honey? Can you give me a hand?"

"Sure," Charles says. "Be there in a second."

After Charles joins Grace in the kitchen, Randy walks around the room. All the furniture is new and matches. When he lived with Charles, they used boxes as an entertainment center and sat on a couch they'd hauled in from the street with ripped seats and exposed springs. But Charles's house isn't just furnished, it's *decorated*. The pillows match the curtains that match the trim on the windowsills that match the rug. Randy's exhausted just thinking about the effort that must have taken.

Charles reenters the room, startling Randy.

"Sorry about that. Women. You know how it is."

Randy takes a big sip and says, "No, actually, I don't."

"You ever even got close? I mean, to getting married? Engaged, even?" He snaps his fingers. "God, remember that girl Sarita from when we lived together? She had the hots for you."

"The problem with 'the hots' is that it goes away. What you're left with is warm, and that's no fun."

Grace calls them to dinner.

The table's set with plates, wine glasses, silverware, napkins, candles, and bread plates. Randy realizes there are more dishes on this table than he owns. As he sits down, Grace enters with a platter filled with roasted chicken covered in herbs. She sets down the platter as Charles fills the wineglasses with Sauvignon Blanc. Grace exits and reenters the room bringing various bowls of food—roasted potatoes, green beans, corn, bread. She finally sits down on the other side of Charles, across from Randy.

"I think that's everything," she says.

"Honey, it all looks delicious."

"Yeah, it looks fucking awesome. Smells good, too."

"Why thank you, Randy."

As they begin to pass around the food, Randy looks at Charles. Within the wrinkles and baldness, Randy can see his old friend.

Grace says, "So, Randy, tell me. What was he like back then?"

"You mean Chipp?"

Hearing his old nickname, Charles smiles bashfully.

"He was a lot of fun. Back then."

Grace touches Charles's hand with the hand that's not holding a fork.

"Don't worry, sweetie. I still think you're fun."

Randy raises his glass. Grace and Charles put down their knives and forks and raise their glasses, too, thinking Randy's going to make a toast. But he doesn't. He just takes a big gulp of wine, sets down the glass, and tears into the chicken.

As they eat, Charles asks Randy what he's been up to the past few years. Randy can tell as he answers that Charles doesn't approve of all of the jobs, or the fact that he still lives in an apartment with roommates. Charles then takes over the conversation, talking about Maddie, his boring job, moving to Tiger Bay. When Charles begins to show photos on his phone from the Trust Christmas party last year, Randy's eyes glaze over.

After dinner, Grace brings out an almond cake. Charles and Grace each have an espresso. Randy keeps drinking wine. When the cake is gone, Grace gets up and begins to clear the dishes. Charles tries to stop her.

"No, honey, let us help."

"She's got it," Randy says. "Let her do her thing."

Grace just grins and shoots Charles a glance that Randy catches.

"Thanks, darling," Charles says. "It was a wonderful meal. Wonderful."

"Wonderful," Randy repeats.

"Thanks, guys. You go and finish your drinks. I'm going to do a little cleaning up and then head to bed. Randy, it was nice to meet you."

Randy just raises his glass. Again, it seems like he's going to say something, but doesn't.

"Shall we retire to the den?"

"Let's," Randy says. Then he burps. "Shall."

Charles and Randy walk back to the den. Randy takes his wine glass while Charles leaves his espresso cup behind. Charles takes a seat in a large blue wingback chair, while Randy straddles a patterned ottoman sitting next to a credenza.

"Seriously, dude, your wife is hot."

"You mentioned that."

"How old is she? She wasn't a virgin when you met her, was she?"

"Randy, let's talk about something else."

"Fine." Randy pouts. He's dying for a cigarette, but is sure Charles wouldn't allow it.

For the next hour they exchange gossip about common friends—where they ended up, who they married, what they're doing now. During the discussion, Randy keeps drinking. He finishes off the bottle of wine and then goes back to whiskey. He can tell that Charles isn't happy about it, but he also doesn't have the balls to stop him. Charles finally looks at his watch and says, "Wow, it's getting late." Randy gets the hint. He digs into his pockets for his keys.

"You okay to drive?"

"Yes."

"Are you sure?"

"Fucking *yes*, Charles. I'm *fine.*"

"Let me call you a cab, okay? Or why don't you—do you Uber?"

Randy pushes Charles out of the way and stomps to the front door. When one of his heels catches on the welcome mat, he's almost sent reeling down the pathway. He catches himself at the last moment.

"Randy, wait." Charles whispers. "Really, Randy. *Stop.*"

Randy gets into his Tercel. He can see Charles out of his peripheral vision as a blur. The neighborhood's eerily quiet. There are no lights on in any windows. Everyone's asleep. When Randy starts up his car, it sounds like firecrackers. He puts it in gear and drives off. In his rearview mirror he sees Charles enter his house and, by the time he turns the corner, it's just in time to see Charles's lights go dark.

As Randy tries to find his way back to the freeway, he marvels at how nice the houses are—so much red brick, so many white columns; mile after mile of shutters painted a variety of dark colors: black, blue, green; so many perfect lawns, gardens with gorgeous flowers, yards hemmed in by white picket fences. Randy thought neighborhoods like this were only in the movies.

He tries to remember how long it's been since he's been in this part of town. Twenty-five years? More? Growing up he'd had a few friends who lived here, rich kids who got into trouble which their parents later got them out of. There were parties where people would drink by the pool until they fell in, or basements where everyone would sneak in the side door and empty rumpus room refrigerators of all of their beer. Someone's parents always seemed to be out of town.

*Those kids didn't have a care in the world.*

At sixteen they each would be given a new car—a BMW or even a Mercedes. At that age all Randy had to get around town was a second-hand bike. It didn't seem fair to him then. It doesn't seem fair to him now.

And now he's lost. He turns around once or twice, but each time he ends up dead-ended on some street that doesn't look familiar. He pulls off to the side of the road.

*That house. That wife. That daughter.*

The car knocks violently twice and then dies.

*Charles's life.*

Randy begins sobbing. He doesn't even realize it's happening until he feels lines of tears marching down his face. He looks into the rear-view mirror and sees bloodshot eyes. But then he focuses on something else. A car approaching, red and blue lights flashing. He wipes his runny nose with his sleeve, leaving a silver streak on the flannel he can see in the dark. He hears the engine behind him stop, a car door opening and closing. Crackle from a police radio. The officer approaches just as Randy finishes rolling down his window.

"Sir, do you know what time it is?"

"It's nearly midnight."

Mark, sweating, looks up at the clock above the entrance to the studio. "God," he says, laughing. "I had no idea."

Steve immediately drops his sticks and stands up.

"Jesus, Robin's going to kill me." As he heads for the door, he's a bit hunched over and walking stiffly. "I'm going to feel this in the morning."

As Gary and Mark take off their guitars and unplug, Gary says, "Same time tomorrow, boys?"

"Yes," Steve says. He already has car keys in his hand and is standing in the doorway. His sweatshirt is draped over his shoulder. "But tomorrow I can only stay until four. We're having Graham's Italian tutor over for dinner."

"Fine. But tomorrow we'll talk about the schedule for the rest of the week. I'd like to get in at least three more practices before Saturday, and we need to finalize the set list, pronto. There's no point in relearning any of these songs if we're not going to play them next week."

"Sure, sure," Steve says as he disappears through the studio doors.

Gary and Mark put their guitars back in their cases and turn off the amps followed by the lights. While Gary locks up, Mark carries his guitar outside. It's never felt heavier.

Their cars are the only ones left on the street. The night is silent, the sky full of stars. Walking to the rental car, Mark can't believe it. In Manhattan you never see stars.

"How did it feel in there?"

Mark pops the trunk, puts the case inside. "Good," he says. "Better than I thought it would." He slams the trunk.

"Yeah, for me, too." Gary throws his bass into the back of the Chrysler. He walks over and leans against Mark's rental car. "You know, at one point I looked over and it was just like old times—me on the left, you on the right, Steve in the middle pounding away. And because we were rusty, and kind of trying to find our groove, it reminded me of when we were first getting started."

Gary's right. That's how it felt for Mark, too.

"Funny thing is," Gary continues, "I don't feel much different now than I did then."

"What do you mean?"

"I mean, I know I'm older. I certainly feel it in my body. But otherwise, I don't know. I still like going out. I like playing loud music and getting high. I still feel like I did back then." He laughs. "I guess that's not good in a lot of respects."

Mark shrugs. He doesn't know what to say. Gary fishes a pack of cigarettes out of his pocket and lights one up. The red tip glows in the darkness.

"By the way, I know how you used to park and wait for Steve at rehearsals." Gary takes a deep drag, holds it in his chest, and then exhales a huge cloud of smoke. "I know it was weird at first because you didn't know me."

"Gary, I never meant anything by that, it's just—"

"Don't worry about it, Pellion. It is what it is. Or was."

After Gary says this, he ashes on the ground and then looks up to the sky.

"We grew to be friends. Over time, I mean. But at first, yeah." Mark laughs. "I avoided you."

"And you're still doing it."

Mark looks from the sky to Gary.

"I've been trying to get in touch with you for years, Mark. I sent emails. I got your address from your dad. You never replied."

"I'm sorry. I just didn't want to get into everything again. I was tired of explaining everything."

"Yeah, but *did* you explain it?" He takes another drag. "Because you never explained it to me."

"Gary, come on. Let's not do this. I can't, really. That was a long time ago."

Gary laughs.

"In a galaxy far, far away." He throws the cigarette into the street and heads over to the Chrysler. "See you tomorrow."

# 4: AS WE GO UP, WE GO DOWN

"How was your weekend?"

Charles looks up and sees Brooks. A coffee cup in his left hand says #1 DAD. On his right wrist is a huge silver watch. Charles just got off the elevator.

"Oh, hey." Charles didn't think anyone would be in this early. Glancing at his own watch, he sees it's just past seven-thirty. "What are you doing here?"

Brooks takes a slow sip of his coffee, looks around.

"I like to get in early. Get a bit of work done before everyone else comes in."

Charles looks around the office, trying to see if Brooks is the only one there. All the lights are off except for Brooks's office and the break room.

"I'd better get back to it," Brooks says. "I'm trying to respond to all of my weekend emails before the conference call at nine."

"Good luck."

Charles watches as Brooks retreats down the hallway, disappearing into his office. Charles goes into his own office. He puts down his bag and takes out his laptop. He sits down at his desk, rethinking the plan he'd come up with yesterday. He'd wanted to get into the office early to dig up some dirt on Dylan, when he didn't think anyone else would be here.

"Hey, Brooks!"

When Charles calls out his voice echoes throughout the empty floor. Brooks appears in the doorway.

"Could you do me a favor? I sent something to be printed on the fourteenth floor. Could you go grab it for me?"

"Why don't you just print it down here?"

Brooks nods to where the printer sits down the hall, sandwiched in a cluster of cubicles that nobody wants to occupy since the printer's old and loud and runs all day.

"I—it's just." Charles can't think of an excuse. Finally, he says, "I need color copies, and that shitty one we have only does black and white."

"Are you sure?" Brooks turns and looks down the hallway. "Because I could swear that—"

"I mean—I *know* it does color copies. I tried that. On Friday." Charles forces a laugh. "And there were yellow spots everywhere. I think it needs more toner. So I sent it upstairs. Could you go get them for me?"

"But, you're—"

"Someone called me when I was in the car and I told them to call me in the office in ten minutes and, well, it's almost been ten minutes."

Charles can tell that Brooks doesn't quite believe what he's saying, but he's still too new at Trust to question him.

"Oh—okay, yeah. Sure. Give me a few minutes and I'll go get them."

"Thanks, man. I appreciate it."

Brooks disappears from the doorway. Charles hears him walk down the hallway and press the button for the elevator. Charles opens his laptop, finds a presentation at random, and sends it to the color printer up on fourteen. The elevator arrives. Charles peeks out his door, making sure Brooks gets on. After Brooks disappears behind the closing doors, Charles sprints down the hallway.

Dylan and Charles have almost the exact same office—desk, credenza, three low filing cabinets under two windows that have a view of the parking lot. There's also a round table in the corner with three chairs.

Charles stands behind Dylan's desk. There's not much on it except a manila folder marked INVOICES and his schedule for the week, which Sharon must have printed out for him on Friday.

Charles quickly goes through Dylan's desk, opening and closing drawers. All he finds are two Mont Blanc pens, a bottle of cologne, and a few expensive chocolate bars. Charles is breathing heavily, sweat forming on his forehead. He goes through the cabinets, finding nothing but company stationery along with envelopes and return address labels, the word TRUST staring back at him from each pile. Turning to the credenza, he sees a photo of Dylan from Disneyworld. Dylan's posing with his two sons. Charles has met them on a few occasions—the summer barbecue, the holiday party, O'Brien's birthday in a backroom at Nolan's.

Knowing he doesn't have much time before Brooks gets back, Charles moves to the filing cabinets. He begins quickly flipping through the various plastic tabs, trying to find something incriminating. As his fingers rifle through the files, he mutters under his breath, "Come on, come on, come on."

Something beeps. At first he thinks it's the elevator—Brooks, maybe, already back—but then Charles realizes it's his phone. It's a text from Grace.

*Maddie has a bit of a fever :-( Am going to stay home with her. Text me on the way home. May need you to pick up some medicine. Love you. Grace*

Charles left the house so early this morning, neither his wife nor his daughter had been awake. Hoping to be the first one at the office, he snuck out of the house before seven.

He quickly texts her back.

*Sorry to hear. Thanks for handling. Love you both. Will check back in a bit.*

A second later Grace writes back with a row of hearts and a picture of Maddie on the couch in her My Little Pony pajamas. Her nose is red and her normally sparkling eyes look dull and glassy.

*She's why I'm doing this. It's for Maddie. And for Grace. For a better life for both of them.*

Charles shoves the phone back into his pocket and returns to the filing cabinets. He quickly pulls out entire folders labeled EXPENSES, BOARD MEETING, and 2012 SALES CONFERENCE. Just as he tucks them under his arm, he hears the ping of the elevator.

Charles quickly jumps into the hallway and walks back to his own office as fast as he can without running. Behind him, he hears Brooks. By the time Charles throws the files onto his desk, and leaps into his chair, he's out of breath. Looking up, he sees Brooks in the doorway. He has the presentation in his hand.

"Your printouts."

Charles reaches out. His chest is heaving back and forth. "Thanks."

After handing over the presentation, Brooks leans against the doorway. "That must have been some phone call."

Before Charles can say anything the elevator pings again. Charles and Brooks turn their heads toward the sound. Voices begin to fill the office, the first waves of workers showing up for a new week.

Brooks sighs. "Well, there goes my whole day."

Randy's been on the computer all morning looking for work, eyes scanning job descriptions and clicking links. It's been four hours and he has nothing to show for it except dry eyes and a sprained thumb. It's all he did yesterday, too. But there's nothing out there. At least, nothing that looks promising. He's been submitting online applications all over town, at dozens of places—it's easy to do; you just upload your résumé and cut and paste a cover letter—but no one's gotten back to him. He's applied for temp work, three telemarketing jobs, and the night shift working security at the mall. The response has been silence. He's not even getting calls for jobs he'd never want.

He looks at his résumé, thinking maybe he left a few digits out of the phone number, or messed up his email address. It wouldn't be the first time. To his surprise he sees that they're both correct. He delves a little deeper.

As he reads over the dozen jobs he's had over the years, he winces. His eyes focus on a restaurant he worked at a few years ago.

*That was a nice place. The tips were good. If I'd just kept my mouth shut, I could have been assistant manager by now.*

Most of the jobs are ones that he left voluntarily. Getting fired the other day was only the second time that's happened to him. Most times Randy just quits, feeling slighted or pissed off about some small thing. He left the record store because he felt the owner had bad taste in music. He quit the bakery because he hated getting up early. He worked in a bank for a while as a teller—it was probably the best job he's ever had, even though he had to wear chinos and a tie—but he left after four months because the bank was located in a crowded strip mall and he had to park two blocks away. The manager even offered to transfer him to another branch, but Randy refused since they were all too far from Kitty—too far for Randy to drive. At the bottom of his résumé, under "Education" all it says is HIGH SCHOOL. Under "Special Skills" it says NONE.

He closes his laptop and looks around for his clock, but still can't find it. He grabs his phone. 11:17. He skipped breakfast and now is looking forward to lunch. But he doesn't have any food in the house.

He sees the printout of the Bottlecap ticket on his desk. Since he doesn't have a printer, he had to ask Cody to print it out for him. Cody wasn't happy about it.

"If you have money to spend on concerts," he'd lectured, "then you'd better have money for the rent."

What kills Randy is that it's true. He can't afford the concert. He doesn't even know why he's going. Dinner the other night with Charles was a disaster. The rich, uptight prick looked down on him the entire night. The only good thing about it was that Randy had managed to talk his way out of a DUI.

He shakes his head. Charles had been his first real friend. They were close in high school, college, and after. They'd been through so much, and now there's nothing. When they shook hands on Saturday, it was like meeting him for the first time. And he didn't particularly like him. If he'd passed Charles on the street, and didn't know who he was, Randy would think he's just another yuppie douchebag. And yet that used to be his best friend.

Randy stares at the receipt for the concert. Now it'll be two meals he'll have to miss. If he stretched it, that $18.50 could have bought him groceries for a week. Now he has less than twenty bucks in his checking account. But that money's already spent since he's going to need gas soon to drive to some interviews, not to mention he'd better get that old suit of his dry-cleaned. Staring down at his bulging belly, he doubts it still fits.

Randy slowly reaches for his phone and dials.

"Mom?"

"Randall, my goodness!" The voice is scratchy but excited. She has to take gulps of air as she speaks, all those years of smoking closing off almost all of her lungs. "How are you?"

"I'm good, Mom. How are—are you good?"

"I'm fine Randall, just fine. I'm on the porch. Can you hear the birds? Your father just bought us cordless phones."

His mom's always at least one technology behind. Now that the whole world has mobile phones, she's finally segued to cordless.

"That's great, Mom. Hey, listen. Could you—could I borrow some money?" Randy says this fast, as if the sentence were like ripping off a Band-Aid.

"But, but I—what about your job, Randall? At the book shop?"

"I lost it, Mom. Last week."

"Oh, Randall. Not *again*."

Disappointment in her voice. Randy's heard it plenty of times.

"Yes, Mom. *Again*. I'm sorry. I made a mistake. Okay, a few mistakes. And now I just need a little bit, a little something, until I can get a new job. I promise—"

"Your father—"

"—that it won't happen again—"

"—made me *swear* to not keeping giving you—"

"—you'll see, Mom."

"—more money. Why, it must have been *thousands* now over the years, Randall."

His head's in his hands. The whole room goes black.

"I know, Mom. I know."

"And, well, it's just not that *easy*, Randall. You must know that. I mean . . ." she loses her train of thought, or can't find the words. Either way, when there's silence on her end he hears birds. It must be sunny in Richmond. It's cloudy in Kitty. "I just don't have it to give."

"Okay, Mom. I just thought you'd—I don't know, Mom."

"Look at your brother, Randall. He's got his own business now. Two locations, even. Maybe you could ask him to—"

Randy hangs up the phone. A minute later his phone buzzes. He turns it off.

For a few seconds, he just sits there. The house is strangely quiet. He gets up from the desk and leaves his bedroom. There's no one in the kitchen or the living room. Randy tiptoes to both Hunter and Cody's doors and, behind each of them, he can hear typing and music playing at a low volume. Randy suspects they're avoiding him, though he doesn't know why.

*I bought Hunter more quinoa and got Cody coffee that had a picture of Africa on it. What more do they want me to do?*

He looks across the kitchen and sees the clock on the microwave. 11:24. Still too early for lunch. Randy's heading back to his room when he spots a wallet sitting on an end table in the living room. It's black and thin. Randy's not sure who it belongs to, Cody or Hunter.

Randy tries to stop, to turn around and go back to his room, but somehow—something's pushing him—he moves forward. He bends at the waist, his movements slow and deliberate. He tries to stop, to scream, to draw some sort of attention to himself so he won't do what he's about to do. But he does it anyway.

He grabs the wallet, lifts it up, and opens it. The first bill he sees is a fifty. The bill disappears, reappearing in his hand, just like magic. The wallet is returned to the table. As Randy walks slowly his room, his eyes fill with tears for the second time in three days.

Mark pulls up to the practice space and parks. The Chrysler from the other day is parked across the street. When he enters the room through the double doors, he sees Gary strumming away frantically on an electric guitar and screaming into a microphone. The sound is loud and distorted. The only words Mark can make out are "fuck," "yeah," and "badass."

When the song's over, Gary turns and notices Mark. When the feedback dissipates, he says, "That's a song for one of my new bands. What do you think?"

"I think you're in your forties and you shouldn't be making music like that."

"What's your problem? I'm just having fun." Gary unstraps the electric guitar and turns off the amp. "Speaking of which, I brought you one of these. It's my new record."

He pulls a cassette out of his back pocket and hands it to Mark. The cover looks like a vintage Polaroid of a beach sunset, with STUBBORN BUBBLES written against the sky in someone's shaky handwriting. Mark opens the cover and pulls out the insert. The edges are uneven, cut by hand. The cassette's a gray Maxwell with SIDE A written in Sharpie on one side and SIDE B on the other.

"Some guy dubbing these in his bedroom, one at a time," Mark says. "That's what passes for a record label these days?"

"Not in the traditional sense, but it gets us out there."

"If by 'out there' you mean 1993, then well done."

"Don't be an asshole, okay?" Gary nods to what Mark's carrying in his hand. "That your acoustic? Good, let's rehearse for the in-store."

As Gary grabs a beat-up Yamaha from a stand and gives it a few strums, Mark hops onto one of two barstools sitting in front of the drums. Gary climbs onto the other.

"You know, Mark, before we get started, I just have to ask." Gary's looking at the guitar while he speaks, tuning it up. "Do you ever think about it?"

"Think about what?"

"Los Angeles. The deal. How our lives would have been different if . . ."

"If what?"

Gary looks up.

"If you hadn't walked away."

Mark shifts uneasily on the barstool.

"No."

"Really?" Gary laughs. "I don't see how you can't since—" But he stops.

"Since what?"

"Well, it's just—it's not like you're such a hotshot in Manhattan. I checked."

"What's that supposed to mean?"

"I Googled you. You design book covers. That's it. There's no other mention of you anywhere. No Facebook. No Twitter. You barely exist. Sure, there're a few things about Bottlecap, from way back in the day, but nothing from now."

"That doesn't mean I don't exist, or that I'm not happy. It just means I'm doing my own thing." Mark strums the guitar. It's out of tune. "What, you think because I didn't become a rock star I'm hiding out and crying myself to sleep every night?"

Gary digs around in his pockets for a cigarette. He finds one. Lighting it, he says, "Basically."

"That's *your* dream, Gary. Not mine." Mark motions around the room, to all of the gear. "And if you want to keep hanging on to it, go right ahead."

"Damn straight, Mark. Damn *fucking* straight." An edge creeps into Gary's voice. "Do you know how many times I've had to watch some shitty band make it bigger than we ever did? I have to open up for them all the time. These fucking kids. I could blow them off the stage any night of the week, but *they're* the ones on tour. The ones with the record deal. And *I'm* opening for *them*. It's not fair. It should have been me. It should have been *us*."

"I'm sorry you feel that way, Gary. But that's just the way things worked out."

"No, Mark." Gary points at him with his cigarette. "That's the way things are because *you* fucked us over."

"Don't give me that. Don't you remember when you wanted to quit the band?"

"What? When?"

"Here, in Kitty. Right before we got the deal. You wanted out and I pulled you back in."

"Why are you bringing *that* up?"

"Because if it wasn't for me none of that would have happened in the first place. The deal. LA. You guys were pretty comfortable there for a while. Videos. Tours. So don't complain now. You guys were fine."

"Fine? We were *fine*, Mark? Wow, that's a real relief to know because it certainly didn't feel *fine* when you went missing just as we were trying to finish the record. It also didn't feel *fine* when we were scheduled to make a video and no one knew where you were. And how *fine* were we when the record company put Steve and me on the hook for completing the tour that *you'd* agreed to? Does any of that sound *fine* to you?"

If Gary says the word "fine" one more time, Mark's going to scream.

"Do you know I called your parents? I called that girl you lived with when we were in LA, Corinne. I even called Laura."

That name again.

"Yeah?" Mark sneers. "And what did *Laura* say?"

"She didn't say anything. She hadn't heard from you, either. She said she wrote you a letter, while we were recording the album, but you never wrote her back."

"Gary, that was a long time ago. Let's drop it. You're lucky I came back to town at all. So don't piss me off by bringing stuff up from the past, okay?"

"I *am* going to keep bringing it up, Mark, because you ruined my life."

Mark turns to look at him. Gary's tearing up.

"I didn't ruin your life, Gary. At least," his voice falters. "I didn't mean to. I just—look, I'm sorry. Is that what you want me to say?"

"For starters, yes."

"Then I'm sorry. I truly am. But the fact is—" Mark notices the guitar in his hand is shaking. "The fact is, we—I—can't go back. Things can't be changed. Where we are in our lives is where we are. What happened to us is just . . . I don't know . . . what was supposed to happen."

Gary laughs and shakes his head.

"God, what a crock of shit. A *total* crock of shit. Maybe you're fine with *your* life not amounting to much, but I'm not." He leans in and puts his cigarette so close to Mark's face he can feel its heat. "Look at you. Hiding in New York. Hiding from life. At least I'm out there. At least I'm still trying."

"What? With *cassettes*? You're practically middle-aged. You should be married and have kids. Own a house."

Gary sneers.

"What, like you?"

The comment sinks in. Neither of them speak. Outside, a car missing its muffler drives by.

"Gary, face it. It's gone. We had our chance."

"Don't say that."

"Why not? It's the truth."

"You're wrong. You fucked it up for all of us and now . . ."

Gary stops. He looks up at the ceiling, then down at the ground. Anywhere but at Mark.

"What?"

Gary just shakes his head. He says, "And now . . . forget it. Let's just worry about this week, okay?"

"Okay."

They each strum their guitars a few times, hitting various strings and finishing their tuning up. Gary finally says, "Ready?"

Mark steadies the guitar and says, "Ready."

Something's happening at Seatr. No one's wearing headphones and no one's really talking. Normally there are a dozen conversations occurring around the room, bits of words and dialogue you can't escape from without putting on the headphones that no one's currently wearing. The only noise is the hollow *tock tock tock* of a Ping-Pong game in the conference room, a beat so steady it sounds like the second hand of some gigantic clock. James has been mowing down people all day, yet Craig's never seen the office so crowded. He looks around and sees coders, interns, even board members. Craig also spots people he doesn't recognize. There are three of them, standing with Josh, huddled in the corner. They're young and dressed like Seatr employees. Jeans, T-shirts, sneakers. Every once in a while one of them looks around the room, points, and then types something on an iPad. Then another nods, points, types, and the cycle repeats itself.

Craig tries to concentrate on his work, but finds it difficult. He's been out of sorts since the weekend, since his lunch with Ashley. As soon as he got home on Saturday he texted her, asking to meet again. He knew it was too soon and that he should have played it cool—especially since she was reticent about giving him her number—but Craig couldn't help it. She surprised him by texting right back, saying it was great to see him and that she was thinking of him, too. All Sunday and Monday he texted and sent flirtatious emails. She flirted right back. Craig even began including sentiments like *Thinking of you* and adding *Kisses,* while she began to pepper her messages with a string of Xs and Os.

He gets out his phone and texts her again.

*Darling. I need to see you. A dinner, a drink. ANYTHING.*

She writes back a few moments later.

*Maybe, dear. Maybe. But when?*

He knows he should take things slow, suggesting drinks or another lunch, but he can't help himself.

*My apartment. During the day. Tomorrow or Thursday. Please.*

He sends the text, hoping that Ashley sees what he's really trying to suggest.

This time there's not an immediate response. He sits there. Minutes go by.

"Craig, my man."

He looks up and sees Josh. He's wearing a T-shirt that says HTTP-STER. Craig puts down his phone.

"Hey, Josh. I—how's it going?"

"Not bad, not bad. Can we talk?"

"Of course."

Josh turns and begins to walk to the Ping-Pong room which is now unoccupied, James has taken a quick breather before moving on to his next victim. Josh enters the room, waits for Craig to walk in, and then closes the door. A flat screen TV mounted to the wall, which they used to use for presentations when this was still a conference room, now shows the leaderboard for the Seatr Open. James is listed at the top. Craig scans for his own name and doesn't see it.

"What's up, Josh?"

"Bit of news, my man. Bit of news."

"Great. Is it about the TSA? Because if we're still hoping to jump on any sort of marketing for summer travel, we'd better get going."

Josh shakes his head.

"Change of plans. It looks like we're going to pivot."

"Fall travel?"

"The board decided that our niche is too marginal. They're pulling the plug and we're being merged with another company. I just can-celled our lease, we're going to sell the computers, and the website will be offline by the end of the week."

"What? But I thought—why?"

"We just weren't gaining traction fast enough. I kept telling you, we needed users."

"And I kept telling *you* we needed the site to actually function."

Josh shrugs.

Craig says, "Okay, but what does this actually *mean*? Who are we being merged with?"

Josh picks up a Ping-Pong paddle from the table and runs his fin-gers over the red rubber padding.

"Pillw. It's another startup based here in the building. Half our board is also on their board. We'll be moving into their offices next week."

"But who are they? What do they do?"

"It's a subscription pillow service."

"*What?*"

"Once a month, they send you a pillow."

"That sounds ridiculous." Craig's voice begins to rise. "Why would anybody want that?"

"Craig, don't overthink it. The board is behind this, you keep your job, and Pillw's got at least another six months of funding. At my last company we pivoted twice before we were successful. Besides, don't complain, you're one of the lucky ones."

"Lucky meaning what?"

"Not everyone's being brought over to Pillw. There'll be some re-dundancies. But don't worry." Josh puts down the paddle and puts a hand on each of Craig's shoulders. "You're going to be fine. Trust me."

Craig's trying to process all of this when the monitor on the wall begins flashing NEXT MATCH in white against a red background.

Josh says, "I wonder who James's next victim is."

Craig suddenly remembers being challenged last week and ac-cepting.

*It can't be. It just can't. For the love of God.*

The door flies opens, slamming against the wall. James enters, holding his special paddle. He has a grin on his face. Half the office follows James into the room. As the Seatr staffers line the walls, even Josh drifts backward and joins the crowd.

"You ready?"

James's voice is low and scratchy. Craig gulps and picks up the paddle that Josh had been holding just a few moments before.

"Uh, yeah—sure."

Craig scampers into place.

One of the coders—Craig's not sure which one—looks at him and says, "Heads or tails?"

"Pardon?"

Josh leans forward. "Craig, it's to see who serves first."

"Oh, right. Right." Craig breathes in deep and, trying to sound as tough as possible, growls, "*Heads.*"

The coder flings the quarter into the air with his thumb. It goes impossibly high, almost reaching the exposed heating ducts hanging from the rafters. Everyone in the room seems to breathe in when it rises and exhale when it falls. The coder catches it, gives it a look, and says with a smirk, "Tails."

James grabs a ball from the bottom of the table, gives Craig an intense stare, and serves in a quick, fluid motion. The ball whizzes past Craig, hitting the wall.

Someone says, "Point."

James serves again. This time Craig manages to return the serve, only to see James fire back the ball so hard it's nothing more than a white blur. When Craig picks up the ball from the ground, it's warm.

James says, "That's two. Your serve."

When Craig hits the ball, it seems to move in slow motion. James grins as he swings. The ball hits Craig in the hand before he has a chance to move. He looks down and sees a red circle where the ball hit him.

"Point."

Craig begins to breathe heavily. As he keeps trying to score a point, but never managing it, he gets hot. In no time sweat begins falling onto the table like raindrops.

*I'm an adult. I'm a grown man. And here I am getting slaughtered in Ping-Pong by some young punk in a Linux T-shirt.*

"Craig." Josh steps away from the wall. "If you need to take a few minutes."

Craig, now panting, waves him away. The coders begin to snicker. Craig hears someone take a photo but, by the time he looks and tries to see who it was, he knows it's too late. It's already on the web. There's probably even footage of this on YouTube that has fifty thousand views. By the end of the day, his heavy breathing will be autotuned.

As he keeps playing, and James keeps winning, all Craig can think of is Ashley. How he wants to be with her again. How badly he fucked up all those years ago. How maybe he can change the past and fix things.

*Ashley. Ashley. Ashley.*

Finally, it's over. James raises his hands in the air while everyone in the room—even Josh—cheers wildly. Craig just stands there, his chest heaving. The monitor on the wall lights up. WINNER: JAMES. LOSER: CRAIG.

The pill breaks in two in her hands. She found it at the bottom of her bag, loose, not even in the prescription bottle. Instead, the pink diamond was just sitting there—stuck, actually—in the crease of the purple patterned satin amid sticks of gum, three Q-Tips, and a pair of earplugs. It's the only pill she could find. But before she could put it in her mouth, it broke in two. She pops the pill—pills—into her mouth anyway. The broken end is jagged and tastes sour on her tongue.

After swallowing, her phone buzzes. A text. Since Saturday Craig's been emailing and texting almost every hour. It started innocently enough with a quick message about their lunch. He thanked her for seeing him again and asked if they might do it again sometime. As the weekend progressed, Craig kept sending messages and Ashley kept responding. Every once in a while she even threw in a word like "dear" or a phrase like XOXO, just for the hell of it.

She glances down at his latest text.

*Ashley, I can't stop thinking about you.*

Without giving it any thought, she types a quick response.

*I know. It's the same for me.*

Seconds later, Craig texts again.

*So then can we get together at my apartment? I'm begging you.*

There's still a part of her, no matter how much she tries to numb herself, that finds it flattering. She knows it's wrong, but she can't help it. It's wiring that's existed for so long, even the Protraxanon finds it difficult to bypass. But whenever she connects the flattery to Craig, and then connects him to her past, the words immediately mean nothing.

The phone in her office rings, but she lets it go to voicemail. A minute later it rings again, and again she doesn't answer it. She sees an email come in from her boss, but Ashley doesn't bother to read it.

A few minutes later, her boss appears in the doorway.

"Oh, Ashley. There you are."

"Yes, Deborah." Ashley sighs. "Here I am."

"I called you and you didn't pick up. And yet I just saw you in the staff meeting, so I knew you were here." Even though her boss says all this in a light tone, Ashley can tell she's annoyed. "Can we chat for a second?"

Ashley gets up and follows Deborah down the hall. In her mouth, where the broken end of the Protraxanon touched her tongue, it still tastes bad.

"Would you mind closing the door?"

Deborah sits down behind her desk. Ashley closes the door and sits down across from her boss. There are photos lining the credenza that stare at Ashley. Deborah with her husband, with her kids, her kids on Halloween. One's dressed as a robot, the other's a pirate.

"So, what are we here to talk about?"

Ashley tries to sound enthusiastic, but it's not terribly convincing.

"I called you in here to talk about Jenna. As you know, she's going to be out for maternity leave starting in a few weeks."

"Yes, and I'm *so* excited for her. Such a *joyous* event, isn't it? Hated to miss the shower the other day. But it's *such* a blessing. So, *so* blessed."

Deborah joins her hands and looks to the ceiling. Ashley thinks for a second that she's going to say a prayer. "This means that we're going to need someone to cover her duties while she's gone. And I was hoping that person would be you."

"Me? Why me?"

"Well, for one thing, I thought the change would do you good. Your recent performance has shown that you're in a bit of a, shall we say, *holding pattern*?"

"But won't giving me Jenna's work in addition to my own be, shall we say, even *worse*?"

"Now, Ashley, there's no need to be sarcastic."

"Well, I'm sorry, Deborah, but this isn't fair. Why not give Jenna's work to Sophie or Bea? They're always just sitting around gossiping anyway."

"Ashley, *please*. I don't think I'm asking for too much. It'd only be temporary and we're *all* going to pitch in. I didn't mean to imply that you'd be handling *every* part of Jenna's job."

Ashley kicks at the desk. She's wearing Tory Burch flats that cost $250. She thought buying the shoes would make her happy. It didn't work.

"Now, Ashley." Her boss's voice is more serious than before. "I've been aware, for quite some time now, that you've been having problems."

"Problems?" Ashley tries to smile, but can't quite manage it.

"Give me a little credit, please. We've known each other a long time. And while you were never a particularly *cheery* person, in the last six months you've become positively morose."

"Positively? Like, in a good way?"

Ashley's phone buzzes. She doesn't look down.

"No, Ashley. *Not* in a good way." Her boss begins to run her hands over the various papers on her desk, flattening them out even though they're already pretty flat. She's doing her best to sound upbeat and cheery, but Ashley can tell it's turning into a struggle. "Frankly, I'd been reluctant to address any of this head-on because I could tell you were in some sort of pain. But now that we're having this discussion, why don't we tackle this? Make this a learning moment?"

Ashley jabs at her stomach, poking at the pill parts to get them to break up, to get them to work.

"In fact," her boss is still, for some reason, talking. "I think we have an opportunity for some real growth here. Yes, I think we can both—"

Ashley hears herself say, "I need to leave."

"What?"

"I don't—feel well."

She stands up. Her feet are moving her toward the door.

Her boss says, "Ashley, I'm sorry to hear that. Do you need to take a few minutes? Do you need some water?"

Instead of answering, Ashley walks out of the office. Deborah calls after her, "Ashley? Are you okay? Ashley?" Her co-workers come to their doors to see what's happening. Sophie. Bea. Jenna with her hand on her belly. Ashley walks stiffly to her office, past them all.

She grabs her purse, picks up the laptop, drops it inside. Her phone rings. She doesn't answer it.

She exits her office and heads for reception, making sure to not make eye contact with Sherry. Ashley makes it to her car, gets in, and checks her phone. The last text wasn't from Craig, it was from Andrew.

*Sweetheart, headed home now. Will make us dinner, so don't get anything on the way home. See you soon. Love you*

She erases the text. She reads the last one from Craig again.

*So then can we get together at my apartment? I'm begging you, my dear.*

She replies.

*Yes. I will meet you. At your apartment. Tomorrow.*


Mark drives to where DISContent used to be, only to discover that it's now something called Gowns and Crowns. Then he remembers that Dave told him DISContent moved to another part of the mall about five years ago. Mark takes a left and then a right, driving deeper into the parking lot toward a section he never visited when he lived in Kitty.

From across the parking lot, he sees it. The DISContent logo sitting in the middle of a huge sign that says on either side: CDS & DVDS and FOR THE RECORD, YES WE CARRY VINYL. This corner of the mall, set far back from Wide Lake Avenue and hidden by the row of stores at the front, seems depressed and rundown. Aside from DISContent, which sits in the corner and takes up half a dozen windows—with merchandise even spilling onto the sidewalk—most of the other stores are small. Mark examines the various signs. GENERATIONS BAKERY

& CATERING. DAZZLES PAGEANTS & PROM APPAREL. HALAL IN-
TERNATIONAL FOOD AND HALAL MEATS.

Despite being tucked away in the corner, the parking lot around
DISContent is crowded. Mark gets nervous, thinking that all the cars
belong to people who are there to see him. He'd been afraid earlier in
the day that no one would show up—that DISContent would be deserted—but now he's afraid of the opposite. He parks the car, lets out
a huge breath, and realizes he's going to play music in front of people
for the first time in decades.

Going through the double doors, Mark can't believe what he sees.
The place is huge. It's at least four times the size it used to be when it
was around the corner. Back then, they had a wall of vinyl and maybe
three aisles of CDs. Now they're selling what looks like an acre of vinyl,
CDs and DVDs, along with T-shirts, posters, headphones, and assorted knick-knacks (some related to music and some not).

In the back, along the far wall, sandwiched between a small section
of musical gear and a wall of kids' toys, there's a stage. Two speakers sit on either side, while four microphones on stands and a pair of
barstools sit in front of a white cinder block wall. About two-dozen
people are lined up around the stage, while another dozen or so are
scattered throughout the store, browsing.

"You're Mark Pellion, right?"

Mark looks and sees a young guy standing next to him. He's wearing a DISContent nametag that says BILLY.

"Yeah. I'm here for the—thing."

"Cool. I'm the manager. Your friend's already back there, getting
set up."

Mark looks and sees Gary stand up from behind a blue sign that
says WATER BOTTLES 2 FOR $10.

"Thanks," Mark says. "I'll go and, uh, get set up, too."

"Great." Billy turns to the store. "This is quite a crowd. I'll tell you,
we never get this many people in here on a weekday."

Mark grins.

*I've still got it.*

Walking away, Billy says under his breath, "Let's just hope they buy
something."

Gary approaches Mark.

"Hey, listen. Before we get started, I just want to say sorry for the other day."

Mark waves his hands.

"Don't worry about it. Obviously there's still some stuff between us."

"Yeah, but—I shouldn't have let it get to me like that. Normally I'm okay. It's just—I don't know. You being back in town has brought out a lot of stuff."

Mark laughs nervously. "I'd hate to think you'd been feeling like that for the past twenty years."

They spot Dave coming in through the double doors. Gary waves at him.

"Oh, don't worry," Gary says. "I *have* been feeling like that for the past twenty years. It's just worse now that you're here."

Before Mark can respond, Dave approaches.

"Fellas, I have good news. The show is *sold out*."

"Holy shit," Gary says.

Mark doesn't know how to react. He's simultaneously happy and terrified.

"Found out last night, just in time to add it to this." Dave unfolds a copy of the *Kitty Courier*, opens it to a page and shows it to Mark and Gary. It's an ad for Saturday's show, featuring a picture of them from 1993. The top says THE ORIGINAL LINEUP, FOR ONE NIGHT ONLY and below that KITTY'S VERY OWN BOTTLECAP. Above the picture a starburst declares SOLD OUT.

"That's fucking amazing," Gary says.

Before Dave can answer, Billy comes up and taps each of them on the shoulder.

"Five minutes, guys, okay?"

Mark sees that the crowd in front of the stage has grown larger. There's no more space, so people trail down the various aisles. Near the entrance Mark spots a TV camera on a tripod, next to a well-dressed woman holding a microphone.

Dave says, "No problem, Billy. We're all set to go. Thanks."

In a daze, Mark climbs onto the stage, gets out the guitar, and makes sure it's in tune. Gary joins him.

"Quite a crowd, eh?"

Mark tries not to get nervous. He swallows hard and does his best to push away the stage fright.

"Yeah, quite a crowd."

Mark and Gary climb onto their barstools. Mark leans forward and says into the microphone, "One—two, one—two."

He hears his voice reverberate through the store. He strums a few chords while Gary does the same. The notes linger in the air. It sounds good. From the front of the store, Billy gives them the thumbs up. Mark looks to Gary. Gary nods. Mark looks at the crowd. Most of them are old, men in their forties or fifties. A few of them look even older than that. Mark spots gray hair, glasses, bald heads.

"Hi, uh, we're Bottlecap."

There's a bit of feedback and then silence until Gary leans forward and adds, "Well, we're two thirds of Bottlecap."

This gets a laugh. The ice is broken.

Gary counts off. They play "Parisian Broke." It sounds really good, the audience clapping when they're done. Gary grins, and even Mark begins to have fun. The woman Gary was talking to before is writing in a notebook and Mark can see a glowing red light on top of the camera. People in the crowd are filming them, too; everyone holds up their phones.

Heads are nodding. People are singing along. It's just like it used to be. There's applause. There's an energy in the air. It feels like the gigs used to feel way back in the day.

But, slowly, a sadness begins to creep into the growing sense of triumph.

*Should I have been doing this all these years? What did I lose when I turned off this part of me? What did I gain?*

Before Mark knows it, they've played the four songs and he's saying "thank you" over and over while the crowd cheers.

As Gary and Mark step off stage, Dave is the first one to approach them.

"Guys, that was fucking awesome." He leans over and whispers in Mark's ear. "There's a newscaster here. She'd like to do an interview. You up for it?"

Mark swallows.

"Sure."

"Great, let me go get her."

Gary leans over, gives Mark a hug.

"That was fucking awesome, man. It really felt like old times. I tell you, I cannot *wait* for Saturday night."

"Yeah." Mark smiles, shyly. "Me too."

Down on all fours, scrubbing the toilet, Craig tries to remember the last woman he had over. No one comes to mind. He recalls a few dinners, and meeting one or two women for a drink, but he never brought any of them home. He dated a bit after he and Gemma split up, once he'd looked up all the women he'd met or been attracted to during his marriage. But none of that went anywhere. Each of the women he contacted told him it was too soon, that he was just rebounding. They all said to "take some time" in order to find out who he "really is."

There was a girl he liked at his last job. They flirted occasionally and, a few weeks after he got the job at Seatr, he gave her a call. She was young but not too young, attractive but not too attractive. Craig thought he had a shot. When he suggested getting together sometime for a bite, she just laughed. "Craig, I don't think of you like *that*." The way she said it made him feel like a fool.

He runs out of Ajax, so Craig just sprays a bunch of Windex into the toilet bowl. Then he takes a shower. Getting out, he pauses to look at his reflection in the mirror. He sees the extra pounds on his hips and gut, the various flabby pouches scattered around his chest and back. When he started at Seatr, he meant to start jogging again. Maybe join a gym. Lose ten pounds. He wanted it to be a fresh start. But none of that happened. He dries off and gets dressed, puts on a pair of new boxers, his designer jeans, and a gingham shirt he ironed that morning.

As he's doing one more round of tidying up in the living room—trying to track down cases for all the loose DVDs scattered on the entertainment center—there's a knock on the door. Craig's heart begins to beat fast. He takes three shallow breaths, runs across the room, and slowly opens the door.

"Hi."

"Hi."

Ashley walks in. Craig takes her purse, only to put it down on the ground right next to where she's standing. She's wearing a knee-length skirt, patterned blouse. Flats. He was hoping for something a bit sexier.

"Did you find the place okay?"

"Yeah." Ashley sits down on the couch. "My gynecologist is right around the corner."

Craig doesn't quite know how to respond to this, so he just shakes his head and offers her something to drink.

"Sure," Ashley says. "Wine?"

"I think I might have something along those lines." Craig tries to sound suave, but even he finds it unconvincing.

When he goes to his small kitchen and gets the two glasses out of the cabinet, all he hears is the sound of glass knocking together. He forgot to put on music. To set the mood.

"Don't tell me," Ashley calls out from the other room. "Your ex-wife took all the furniture."

Craig reenters the room. He hands Ashley her wine. When he does she pops something into her mouth, takes a sip, and swallows.

"What makes you say that?" he says.

"Probably because I'm the only thing in the room *not* from Ikea."

"I just wanted to start over, you know? Not have a lot of stuff that had a bunch of emotional attachments to it."

Craig doesn't know where to sit. Right next to her on the couch seems too close, too presumptuous. But in the chair across the room is too far away and awkward. So he just stands there, sipping his wine.

"Yeah, but *this* stuff looks just like your dorm room at college." She takes another sip. "And for God's sake, will you sit down?"

Craig takes a quick sip and then sits down next to her.

"Listen, Ashley. Thanks for coming over. It's great and I—it means a lot to me. To see you again. You're all I've been thinking about since Saturday."

Ashley nods, sips her wine.

"And, well, it's just great. To see you again. And I just—well, I want you to know that."

"That's great, Craig." When Ashley speaks, her voice sounds almost robotic. Craig thinks back to the lightness she used to have, how she would almost glow. Now she seems different. Dulled. "So, have you lived here a long time?"

"Yeah," Craig says. "Few years now. I moved in here right after the divorce."

"Must have been hard."

"It was. I felt like a failure for a long time. Like I'd let down not just Gemma and my parents, but myself, too. But, you know, you have to pick up the pieces of your life and move on."

"No, I meant the move. *That* must have been hard." Ashley motions to the door with her wineglass. "Lots of steps. Skinny hallways."

Craig finishes his drink in one big gulp. It instantly goes to his head. He meant to have lunch, but didn't.

"So, do I get a tour, or what?"

"Sure. Well, this is the living room/dining room combination."

Craig points to his entertainment center, on top of which sits the cheapest flat screen TV you can buy on the American market. There are cabinets below for stereo components and CDs, but all of that stuff is in storage. All he has is the cable box and a DVD player. The dining room table only has two chairs, which he never thought was depressing until that very second.

"Wow, Craig. You've done really well for yourself."

"Ash, please."

"Don't call me Ash."

"I'm getting my life back together, Ash. It wasn't easy, you know." Craig starts to panic.

*This isn't going the way I wanted.*

"I'm sorry," he says. "I didn't mean to snap."

She drains the last of her wine and sets the glass on the floor.

"Why don't you show me the rest of the place?"

Craig gets up. He leads Ashley back toward the door, and then down the hallway.

"There's the bathroom. And here . . ." He steps aside and lets Ashley walk in front of him. "Here's the bedroom."

Ashley stops at the doorway. There's nothing in the room except a bed and a nightstand. Above the bed, centered on the wall, is a nail with nothing hanging on it. Ashley steps into the room. Craig follows her. When she turns to face him, he takes her in his arms and kisses her. Her mouth is so dry his tongue gets stuck on her teeth. But he keeps going, kissing and inching her closer and closer to the bed.

Opening one eye, he notices that the blinds are up. Sunlight streams into the room. Craig kicks himself for not lowering them earlier. The room is bathed in light, which only serves to remind them that it's the middle of the afternoon and they really shouldn't be doing this. But they don't stop. As she unbuttons his shirt, he looks down and watches her hands. He didn't notice this the other day, at lunch, but they look old. Each hand has wrinkles and dots he suspects are age spots.

"Kiss me." Ashley says this with no trace of romance. Her eyes are closed and, between the paleness of her skin and the sun on her body, she looks like a cadaver. Craig lowers her to the bed and unbuttons her blouse. Her bra clasps in the front, with a little bow in between the cups. He takes off the bra and unzips her skirt, pulling it down inch by inch. He rolls down her stockings and then slides off her panties. Her eyes still closed, the light still harsh, and now fully naked, she looks even more like a corpse. She repeats, "Kiss me."

"Get off me."

Craig rolls over, sinking into the mattress. Ashley pulls up the sheet, covering herself. The light's barely changed. Ashley feels a wet spot on her thigh, already drying.

Craig says, "Sorry I was so quick."

Ashley shrugs. The whole thing lasted less than ten minutes.

She looks over and sees him smiling. That stupid grin. The one that got her into this mess. She says, "What's so funny?"

"I'm just—I don't know."

"What? Spill it."

She kicks him under the covers. Hard.

"It's just—I'm glad we're back together again. Well, not *together*, together, but we're in each other's lives. We have, you know," Craig points to the bed, "this."

"Craig, I don't know what you think *this* is. I don't really know what it is, either. But we are *not* back together."

"I know, I know. But I want to see you again. I want to spend time with you. I want you to be mine. Again."

Ashley pulls away from him slowly.

"Why?"

"Because I still love you."

She closes her eyes, tight. She wishes she could do the same thing with her ears.

"Ash?"

"For fuck's sake, stop *calling* me that."

"I love you, Ash."

Ashley stares out the door, into the hallway, her back to Craig.

"I'm sorry, Ash. To have said that. It's too soon, I know. I'm just happy to see you again. I don't have a lot in my life so this—you— mean a lot to me."

"Craig, I can't—I'm not going to lead a double life. I barely have energy for the one I have now."

He leans in, kisses her neck and then her shoulder, planting kisses up and down her back. She pulls away.

"Fine, you don't want to do the part-time thing," he says. "I get that. So why don't we make it more permanent?"

"What are you saying?"

"I'm saying—I don't know. Let's give it a shot. You know, try again."

"What about Andrew?"

Craig shrugs.

"I don't know. He leaves. Or you leave."

Ashley thinks of their mortgage. The joint bank account. Life insurance. All of the paperwork that'd be involved. She doesn't think she could handle it.

"Craig, I don't think you've really thought this through."

"No, Ash, I haven't. But is that such a bad thing? My god, look at us. Look at the lives we're leading. Why not try for something else?"

"What? With each other?"

"Yes." Craig's voice rises. He's getting excited. He was like that a lot in his twenties. She wonders how often he's like that now. "What's stopping us?"

"You can't be with me right now. You just—can't."

"Look, I know Andrew's still in the picture. I'm fine with that. For a little while, anyway."

"That's not just it. There's—other stuff."

"Like what?"

"Like lots of stuff." She pulls the sheet up to her chin. "For example, my job. I hate my job."

"That's—it?"

"For starters, yes."

"Ash, that's not bad."

"I told you, don't call me Ash."

"Ash, that's *great*."

"How is that great?"

"It means we can both make a clean start."

"What are you talking about?"

"You think I like *my* job? Working inside a never-ending Ping-Pong tournament with people half my age? Besides, we just got sold, or merged, or something."

"What are you saying?"

"I don't know, I'm saying—I don't like my job. You don't like your job." He looks around the room. "This place means nothing to me. My lease is month to month. So why don't we—"

"What? Why don't we *what*?"

"Try to get it right."

"And what does *that* mean, exactly?"

He rubs his chin.

"I guess you're right. I haven't thought it through that far. But we could go away. We could leave Kitty at the very least. Find a new place to live. Get new jobs. Get new lives. Be new people."

Her body tightens.

"Craig, this is only the second time I've seen you in decades, and we didn't exactly end things back then on a high note."

"I'm sorry. You're right. How about—maybe we just meet up on Saturday night, and see how it goes. Okay? My work's having a party."

Finally, the light in the room changes. It's darker now.

"Party?"

"Yeah. For the merger. It's sort of a meet and greet thing. Some of our people, some of theirs. I have to go."

"Yes, but *I* don't have to go."

"That's what I missed, Ash. Your sense of humor."

"Don't call me Ash."

"So then, will you?"

"Will I what?"

"Go with me to the party?"

She considers this.

"Fine," she says. "I'll see you on Saturday."

As he pulls up to Dave's, Mark sees the white Chrysler with the zombie bumper sticker. He parks behind it, gets out, walks to the front door. The letters and fliers scattered on the ground from the other day have multiplied since his visit last week. Mark knocks on the door and, when he answers, Dave doesn't look happy.

"Mark, uh. Hey."

"Dave, sorry to drop by unannounced, but I just wanted to talk to you about the show. Got a second?"

Without waiting to be asked in, Mark enters the house. He finds Gary standing in front of the dining room table. Gary turns when he sees Mark, his arms spreading out, fast, like he's trying to hide something.

"What are you doing here?" Gary says.

"I just came by for a quick chat with Dave before tomorrow. What are you doing here?"

Gary doesn't answer. He just looks at Dave. Dave just looks at the floor.

"Can someone please tell me what's going on?"

When neither of them answers, Mark approaches the table. Gary makes a half-hearted attempt stop him, but Mark just pushes him aside. On Dave's table there's a glossy color print out of the artwork for

Bottlecap's final record. The one the guys finished without Mark. But something's different. On the front, at the top, it says REMASTERED. At the bottom, in a font meant to look like handwritten scrawl, it says SPECIAL '90S SLACKER EDITION.

"What the hell is this?"

When Gary speaks there's wariness in his voice, as if he'd really rather not be speaking. "Next year's the twentieth anniversary of the Bottlecap record. The major label one."

"Yeah, so?"

"So, a label bought the rights to it a few years ago. They got in touch with me last year, and I've been working with them to put out a deluxe edition."

"Deluxe edition, what do you mean?"

"You know, remastered. Digital, CD, even vinyl. And with B-sides, some live tracks. Stuff like that."

"You can't do this, Gary. You can't just put out our record again. Without my—"

"It was never *our* record to begin with, remember? It wasn't exactly a great deal you signed. The label owned everything we ever did."

As Mark stands there, trying to process what's being said, Gary adds, "We're also going on tour."

"As what, one of your shitty bands?"

"No." Gary says this calmly, not taking the bait of Mark's insult. "As Bottlecap."

For a few seconds, there's nothing but silence.

"You can't do that. Bottlecap was *my* band. I started it."

"It's not yours anymore, Mark."

"What's not mine?"

"The band. The name, I mean. Bottlecap. I own it."

"How did—when did that happen?"

"Last year. I got a lawyer. Remember when you signed some stuff for the digital release of the early singles?"

Mark remembers getting a bunch of contracts in the mail from Dave. It was a huge stack of paper, with plastic arrows stuck every other page showing where to sign. Mark signed.

"That was from Dave. That wasn't from you."

Mark looks at Dave. Dave's still staring at the ground.

"I'm sorry, Mark. I wish there'd been another way."

"Fuck you, Dave." Gary's voice now has that edge to it, the same as from the other day. "This is going to be good for both of us."

"Gary, what did I sign?"

"You no longer have any legal right to the name Bottlecap. I told you, I own it."

Mark shakes his head.

"Yeah, but they're *my* songs."

"They *are* your songs, Mark. Which means you're going to get a slice of all this. There'll be royalties and, who knows, we may even license a song to a TV show or a commercial. We're doing a bunch of European festivals, there's an indie rock reunion cruise, and we have three weeks of dates scheduled in the UK. The NME's talking about making us their 'retro band of the week.'"

"But—I was the singer."

"*Past* tense. Hanes is going to be the singer. Again."

"That guy from Los Angeles?"

Gary nods and says, "We did two tours with him after you walked out on us. I looked him up a while ago and he's still—"

"Wait a second." Mark laughs. "Is *that* what this is all about? You're still mad about LA?"

"I told you before, I'm tired of opening for other bands. I'm tired of watching it happen to everyone else but me." Gary makes a ball with his left fist and pounds his chest with it. "This is my chance. You fucked it up last time. I won't let you fuck it up again."

Mark looks around the room. He can't believe any of this is happening.

"You can't do this, Gary."

"It's done, Mark." Gary points to the artwork on the table. "The rerelease is ready to go. The tour's booked. Hell, we even got our T-shirts early."

Mark notices a huge pile of Bottlecap T-shirts in the corner.

"I thought those were just for Saturday."

Gary just grins.

"For fuck's sake," Mark says. "When were you going to tell me all of this?"

"I don't know," Gary says. "Any time after tomorrow tonight, I suppose."

Mark now turns to Dave. "Were you in on this, too? Is the entire benefit some big lie?"

Dave finally looks up.

"It's like I said. It's for the label. But it's not for new bands or new records. I'm going to use the money to repress your early stuff to coincide with the reissue and the tour." Dave stops for a second and grins, like he's impressed with himself. "They're taking me with them. To sell the merch."

"*Merch*?" Mark spits out the word. "Dave, you're over forty. People your age shouldn't use words like 'merch.'" Mark turns back to Gary. "And Steve's in on this, too?"

"Steve's a businessman. He knows it'll be good publicity for the dealership."

"And he knew about all this? The reissue? Buying the name?"

"It was his lawyer who drew up all the papers."

Mark begins to pace back and forth. He's trying to put the various facts in some sort of order so they make sense. "But if this is all set in motion," he says, "and I can't stop it, why did you even need me to come back to Kitty? What's this weekend even for?"

"I had a feeling Steve would be rusty as shit," Gary says, the edge still in his voice. "And Hanes can't get here until June. I figured this would be a good way to get me and Steve back in sync, not to mention test the waters a bit. See what the reaction would be. I'm sorry you had to find out this way, but now that the cat's out of the bag, let's just move on. We don't need to let any of this affect the show tomorrow."

"The show?" Mark says. "You think *that's* still going to happen?"

Gary looks at Dave, who looks scared.

"There's no way in hell I'm going to play with you pricks after you've been doing this shit behind my back."

Gary's calm when he speaks.

"Of course you will, Mark."

"And why would I do that?"

"Because half the town's going to be there tomorrow. To see us. To see *you*. All of our old friends. Reporters. Your parents." He pauses. "*She* might even be there."

"What's that supposed to mean?"

"Mark, don't play dumb. Why the hell else would you come down here again? Lord knows it wasn't for us."

"You think I came to Kitty for Laura?"

"Bull's-eye."

Mark steps forward. He wants to take a swing at Gary, but doesn't. Instead, he balls up his fists so tight his nails dig into his palms.

"Mark," Gary says. "It doesn't really matter what happens tomorrow. Walk out if you want to, but everything else is still happening. It's going to be twenty years since the record came out, no matter what you do. The reissue, the tour, you can't stop any of it."

"I can get a lawyer. I can try."

Gary laughs.

"You do that. The press will help."

Mark begins walking backward. His hands, reaching behind him, find the doorknob. He gives it a twist and then a pull. He feels the breeze from outside on his cheek.

"You guys can both go fuck yourselves."

As he slams the door, he hears Dave call out something. Mark walks briskly to his car. He gets in, starts up the engine. As he pulls away from the curb, he clips the rear of Gary's Chrysler with his front bumper. The white car's pushed first onto the sidewalk and then Dave's lawn. Bits of broken glass from both cars scatter everywhere. Mark heads for the freeway.

Randy's holding a bag of groceries in one hand and digging into his back pocket, looking for his keys with the other. When he enters the house, he sees Cody and Hunter sitting at their usual spots at opposite ends of the kitchen table. But they're not typing, they're just sitting there. Music, for once, is not coming out of either of their laptops. When Randy places the bags of groceries onto the floor, a package of hot dogs falls out and hits the tile with a wet slap.

"Hey guys," Randy says.

Not looking up, Cody says, "We need to talk."

"Okay, shoot."

"Randy, we think you should move out."

"What, why? Because of the rent?"

"Because of a whole lot of reasons." Cody speaks slowly, his words sounding rehearsed. "You know this isn't a great situation—it never has been—so let's just end it now with no hard feelings."

Randy just stands there. He doesn't know if he should sit, stomp out of the house, or do what he was planning to do when he got home: put his groceries away.

"If this is about money, you know I got laid off." His voice has the same shake it had last week when he was in Bill's office at Bookstorage. "How am I supposed to pay rent with no job?"

"That's not really our problem, is it?"

"But you're both doing well. Couldn't you cover me for a while?"

"We could, but we won't."

"Why not?"

"That wouldn't be fair to either one of us. Or, quite frankly, to you." Cody finally looks up. When he does, Randy wishes he'd go back to staring straight ahead. "Look, I realize this has always been a bit of a weird situation. We weren't expecting someone like, well, *you* when we were looking for a housemate."

"You mean someone my age? God, you act like it's a handicap or something."

"A handicap would have been better." Hunter speaks for the first time. "Put in a ramp and, boom, you're done."

"I'm sorry, guys. I'm in a bit of a rough patch right now, that's all."

"*This* is a rough patch?" Cody laughs. "It's been rough ever since you moved in."

Randy wants to defend himself, to tell Cody and Hunter that they're wrong, but he doesn't know what to say. They're right.

"Please, guys. *Please.* Just a little more time."

Cody's shaking his head.

"No, Randy."

"I'm going to get another job, I promise. I've been applying to places all over town and I think—"

Cody cuts him off.

"For God's sake, Randy, you stole from us."

He says, weakly, "What, me? Never." He knows it's not convincing.

Cody grabs his phone and checks it. "Look, today's the seventeenth. Why don't we make a clean break of it and have you out by the first, okay? You paid your last month's rent when you moved in, so let's just say that's the rent you owe for this month."

Randy says quietly, "What about my security deposit?"

"I'm afraid I'm going to need that to cover all the money I've lent you since you've been here."

"Guys, you can't just throw me out on the street. I don't have a job. Where am I supposed to go?"

"That's not really our problem, now is it?"

"*Please.*"

Neither Cody nor Hunter respond.

As Randy stands there, shell-shocked, his stomach grumbles. Since being laid off, he's only been eating two meals a day. He looks at the clock. 3:46. He had half a bowl of Apple Jacks when he woke up, and nothing since then.

"Okay," he says. "I'll go."

Cody and Hunter sort of nod and stand up, taking their laptops into their respective rooms. Randy feels the grumbling again, his stomach empty, wanting food.

He looks at the clock.


3:47. Still no word from Tom. After going through Dylan's files at home on Monday night, holed up in his office for hours while Grace and Maddie wondered what he was doing, Charles didn't find anything incriminating. Panicking and needing something to send to Tom, he created dozens of incriminating documents. Inflated expense reports, damning email chains where Dylan and Sharon trashed O'Brien, and a series of notes that implied they were sleeping together. Charles dropped off everything at Tom's office on Tuesday morning, but hasn't heard anything since.

He spent the rest of the week in a cold sweat. He canceled his meetings and, when Brooks stopped him in the hall and asked what was the matter, Charles just pointed to his belly and muttered something about not feeling well. It was the truth. His stomach has been folding in on itself all week. On Wednesday, Dylan and Sharon went missing. They were both there in the morning but, when Charles came back from lunch, they were gone. People asked about them—wondering if they'd be back, asking why they left in such a hurry—but no one had any concrete answers. By Thursday afternoon rumors started flying and, by the end of the day, people were looking at Charles in a strange way. When he walked around the office, conversations stopped. Even Brooks wouldn't make eye contact. Now it's almost the weekend, and Charles still doesn't know what's happening.

Most people on the floor have already left. A few offices still have their doors open, but the cubicles are all empty. The photocopier is rhythmically chugging, someone printing out something for Monday morning. Once spring arrives, Fridays are a ghost town. Charles could have left hours ago. He's only sticking around in case Tom wants to see him.

When his phone rings, just before five, Charles jumps. It's Heather.

"Can you come by for five minutes with Tom?"

"Of course I can."

He gets up and slowly walks to the elevator. Brooks passes him, his arms full of files. When Charles says, "What's up?" Brooks doesn't respond.

Up on sixteen, the floor's just as empty as downstairs. As Charles approaches Tom's office, Heather waves him in. Tom's behind his desk. He motions for Charles to close the door, so he does. When Charles turns back, Tom says, slowly, "So, how's my new VP?"

"What? *Me?*"

"Don't act so shocked. I just met with O'Brien, and it's official. You're in." Tom's grinning from ear to ear. "I thought you'd want to know before the weekend."

When Charles sits down, he's shaking.

"Wow, Tom, this is great. Thanks. Thanks so much."

"Listen, I also wanted to call you up here to go over some of the particulars for the transition, okay?"

"Sure."

"Let's figure on there being a short announcement as part of the next management meeting—which you'll now be attending—and we'll get O'Brien's assistant to write up a memo, pretending that it's from O'Brien, of course, welcoming you to the team. And then we'll put something in next month's Trust newsletter for the other regional offices. Plus, and this is of course the best part, the new salary will kick in after your next paycheck. Does that all sound like a plan?"

Charles can't really believe any of this is happening. He says, "It all sounds great."

"Obviously a lot of people—especially down on twelve—already know that something's up. What with Dylan being, well, gone."

"So, he's gone? As in, *out*?"

"I mean gone as in *fired*."

"Dylan's fired?"

"Of course, Charles. What did you think was going to happen?"

"I don't know. That he wouldn't get the promotion. That he'd just stay where he was." Charles knows that he's speaking fast, that there's panic in his voice, but he can't help it. "I thought that he'd get my duties and I'd become a VP, rather than the other way around."

"Charles, come on." Tom leans forward, his hands clasped. "You can't expect us to keep Dylan after what you dug up on him. He had to go. You showed us that."

"Me?"

"Yes, *you*. And don't think that O'Brien will forget that. Of course, since we had to get rid of him immediately, things will be a bit fucked in the interim."

"No two weeks' notice?"

"Not a chance. We're talking 'fired with cause.' O'Brien actually wanted to bring him up on charges. Said that what he'd done was tantamount to embezzlement. I don't remember the exact phrase, but he was pissed, let me tell you." Tom stops, reconsiders. "I think 'betrayed' was the word he used."

"Betrayed," Charles says. The word rings in his ears.

"No severance, either."

Charles turns from Tom to the window, except this gives him vertigo, so he just stares at the ground.

"Anyway, this means you'll have to do his job, in addition to yours—and all your new duties—until we find a replacement."

"Me?" Charles says again, his voice cracking. "What about Sharon? Why can't she have some of Dylan's work?"

"That fucking cunt? We fired her, too."

"What? *Why*?"

Tom laughs. This is so simple for him, why isn't it for Charles?

"She was an accomplice in the whole situation, Charles. She should have stepped forward. Should have told someone what was happening. Instead, she kept her goddamn mouth shut. Not to mention fucking him at the sales conference. That was just beyond the pale."

Charles just sits there. He doesn't know what to say.

"Listen, I know this is a lot to take in right now. It's been a big week for you. But I need to know I can count on you." Tom looks at Charles and speaks slowly. It only adds to Charles's impression that this is all a dream. "Do you understand? I need to know that you can handle this."

Seconds go by. Charles realizes he's not saying anything, and that he probably should.

"I can," he finally says. "I can handle. This."

Tom breaks his stare, goes back to speaking in his normal voice.

"Good, I'm glad to hear that. Anyway, I just thought you'd want to hear the good news."

"Thanks, Tom. I appreciate it."

"No worries, Charles. Thank *you*."

Charles gets up, and so does Tom. Tom offers his hand and Charles makes sure his grip feels like steel. Their hands interlock. Charles's grip is firm. Tom's hand feels like stone. All is right with the world.

150

# 5: HERE'S WHERE THE STORY ENDS

REQUIEM FOR A SCENE

Mark's on his bed reading the article Seth, the writer he talked to last week, wrote about tonight's show. It's a big story with lots of photos from back in the day. Press shots of Bottlecap, the Deer Park, and the Disappointed cover two interior pages of the *Weekend* section. Dave gets a picture, too—a recent one from inside his house. Stuff's everywhere and his belly's sticking out from an old Violent Revolution T-shirt that's too tight. There's even a tease for the story on the front page, right below the fold. *Rock-and-roll nostalgia hits Kitty*. As soon as Dave texted saying it was on the newsstand, Mark's dad went out and bought every copy. People have been calling all day.

When Mark woke up this morning, he wasn't even sure there was going to be a show. After storming off from Dave's yesterday he got onto I-95 and drove until he cooled off enough to go home. It took about a hundred miles. Finally, realizing he couldn't do that—not to his parents, not to their friends, not even to Gary and Dave—he turned around and headed back. He may have let everyone down once, but he wasn't going to do it again.

Now he's sitting on his bed, the show's just a couple of hours away, and he's reading about himself in the *Times-Dispatch*. Even though Mark finds parts of the story hard to read—there's six paragraphs about him walking out on the band in LA, Bottlecap's ensuing success, and Mark's ensuing silence—it's all handled in a fair way. It's his past. It's his life. There's nothing he can do about his history now.

More interesting is the write-up on the guys from the other bands. The ones who haven't lived in Kitty for years are flying in from all over to play the show; Seth seems to have talked to them all. Most of them are married; some even have kids old enough to come to the show. The drummer for the Deer Park, who everyone used to call Stoner for obvious reasons, is now an entrepreneur in Boston. He got rich on Internet stocks in the late nineties. He's flying down in his private plane. None of them make music anymore, not even as a hobby. One guy sold all his guitars and had to teach himself how to play again. Another's married with four kids, and no one in his family—not even his wife—knew he'd been in a band. And then there's Gary, still trying to cash in on the rock-and-roll dream. Mark doesn't know whether to feel sorry for him, or envious. Who knows? Maybe it'll work. Maybe they'll be some sort of stars (Bottlecap 2.0). Stranger things have happened.

"Son? Look what I found."

Mark puts down the paper and looks up. He sees his dad standing in the doorway. He's wearing clunky black shoes, gray slacks, blue short-sleeve buttoned-up shirt and a wide tie covered in purple chevrons.

"The tie, son. The tie." He looks down, grabs where it forms an angle at the tip, holds it close to his eyes. "Was in the very back of my closet—haven't worn it in years. But I knew I still had it. Don't you remember?"

"Remember what?"

"*You* gave it to me. The first Father's Day you spent your own money. You were ten. Even wrapped it yourself. I'd never been more proud."

"Wow." Mark laughs. The tie's pretty hideous. "I had bad taste as a kid."

"It's for your concert. We're coming to see you, son." His dad continues to fiddle with the tie as he speaks—adjusting it, turning it over, rolling it up. "Never managed to see you back in the day. Thought I'd missed my chance."

"Thanks, Dad." Mark looks down at the paper. His younger face stares back at him. "I just hope you—I just hope it's what you always thought it'd be."

His dad looks up, smiling. Mark can't remember him ever looking so happy.

"How can we not like it? It's *you*, Mark."

When he turns back to the paper, to finish the story, his old digital clock across the room catches Mark's attention. 6:34.

"Shit, I didn't know it was so late." He grabs his wallet and the keys to the rental car. "Dad, look, I'll see you guys there, okay? I need to make a quick stop on my way to the show."

Mark passes his dad on the way out of the room. When he does, he smells aftershave. Bay Rum.

"Okay, son. Okay. Good luck and—well, I'm proud of you."

By the time he says this, Mark's already at the bottom of the stairs.

Ashley's standing at the top of the stairs. She thinks Andrew's home, but isn't sure. It's Saturday, so he can't be teaching. But he might be at the library. He might be in the living room, reading a book. She doesn't know. Ashley slept most of the day, getting out of bed once to pee and then, an hour ago, to shower and get dressed for the party at Craig's office. And now she's standing at the top of the stairs.

As she starts to walk—lightly, trying not to make noise—she notices the wall lining the staircase is bare. This is where families put pictures—portraits, school photos, holiday snapshots. But she and Andrew have put up nothing.

*We've been places. Hawaii. Paris. The Caribbean. Those were good times. Where's the record of that?*

She walks down the hallway, her high heels making noise she wishes they wouldn't. She considered wearing ballet flats, but when she tried them on she thought they looked too young, too hip. Two things she knows she's not. Peering into the kitchen, she looks for evidence of a meal being prepared, or one already consumed. But there's nothing.

It isn't until she enters the kitchen that she finally hears something. A computer. Typing. Andrew's home, in his office, working on his novel.

153

"There you are, sleeping beauty."

She must have made noise, or Andrew spotted her, or both. Ashley walks towards Andrew's office.

He says, "Did you have a good rest?"

"What's that?"

"You've been asleep all day."

"Oh, *that*." Ashley tries to fake a laugh, but nothing comes. Instead, she pats her bag and says, "I—I'm going to the office."

"But it's Saturday." He looks back to his laptop, checking the time. "And it's almost seven."

"Oh, yeah. I *know* it's Saturday. Night. I didn't mean *for* work—like, to *do* work."

Ashley begins to panic. She didn't think he was going to question her. She thought he'd just tell her to have a good time and that'd be it. She didn't even know he was home.

"Then why are you going?"

"What? Oh, they—they're having a dinner. For Jenna. At the office."

"The office? Why not at a restaurant? This is—what—a going-away party? Because of her pregnancy?"

Ashley winces when he says the word. But she fights it. Keeps going.

"Yes, it's a going-away party. For her, because of the—you know. And it's at the office because there's going to be games. Cake. All kinds of stuff."

"I thought they already had a shower for her."

"They did. Last week. This is different. This is—dinner."

"Where are they going to get the food? Or are you all just going to raid the refrigerator in the break room for leftovers?"

"It's a potluck, Andrew, okay? Everyone's bringing something."

"What are *you* bringing?"

"Me?"

"Yes, *you*. You wouldn't want to arrive empty-handed."

She's kicking herself for not thinking this out more clearly.

"I was planning—I'll stop at the Food Lion and get some potato salad or something. A pie, maybe."

"And that's what you're wearing?"

Ashley looks down. She has on a black cocktail dress she hasn't worn since a New Year's Eve party four years ago.

"Well—it's Jenna. She *is* having a, you know, *baby*."

Andrew closes his eyes and raises his hands.

"Please, stop. Your boss called. I know about the other day."

Ashley leans against the doorway for support.

"She wanted to see how you were doing. She was concerned. When I asked what she was talking about, she told me what happened."

"What, exactly—what did she say?"

"She said you walked out of some meeting on Tuesday and haven't been back since. She said that every morning you've left her a voice-mail saying you're not feeling well and that you also haven't returned any of her calls. She says she doesn't know what's going on with you, but she's worried."

When Ashley speaks, her voice is barely a whisper.

"It wasn't a meeting."

"What's that?"

"It wasn't a meeting, Andrew. Okay?"

"Then what was it? What happened?"

"I just needed a break. That's all."

"But then what have you been doing all week? Where have you been?"

"Been?"

"Yes. Every morning you got up, got dressed, and left the house. I thought you were going to work, but I guess not." Andrew shakes his head again and laughs. "And at night, when I asked you about your day, you told me things that happened at the office. You told me about the work you were doing. You were specific. You mentioned details. You told me about people. Conversations. What *was* all that?"

"Those were lies, Andrew. Don't you know when I'm *lying* to you?"

"I guess not." He hangs his head. "Marriage does that. Trust builds up, whether or not you even want it to. Like plaque on teeth."

The phone in her purse buzzes. Andrew notices.

"Is that him?"

"Who, him?"

"I don't know. But if you've been lying about going to work, who knows what else you've been lying about."

"Do you think—" Ashley can barely play this game. "Do you think I could lie about something like *that*?"

"I don't know anymore." He says this more to himself than to her. "I guess I really don't know anything."

"Andrew, please—you've been good to me." She picks at a patch of white paint in the doorjamb. It chips off, falling to the floor like snowflakes. "I know I wasn't what you wanted."

"You were, Ashley. That's what's so sad. You *are* what I want, for as long as I've known you. And I just don't understand why you can't get past—"

"Andrew, drop it. Don't you dare bring that up. Not now."

"Ashley, why are you still hanging on to that? Can't you see it's getting in the way of everything?"

Ashley doesn't answer. She just picks at the wall. The ground at Ashley's feet is now littered with little bits of paint. Trying to change the subject, she says, "Your book, Andrew. Your novel."

"What about it?"

"I never asked. Does it have a happy ending?"

"Of course it does, Ashley. It's fiction."

When she turns to leave, he doesn't stop her.

As she walks toward the front door, the sound of her heels on the hardwood floors echoes throughout the quiet house. She gets into her Prius and looks into her purse. She grabs the amber bottle of Protraxanon and empties it into her left hand. There's just one pill left. She never called the doctor back from last week. After this pill, she's on her own. In the twilight coming through the windshield, the pill seems to glow. She pops it into her mouth.

The party at Seatr's in full swing. Food and drinks are everywhere, Tequila bottles, six-packs of beer, margarita mix. Bags of chips, pretzels, open boxes of pizza. A bunch of kids stand around, all wearing sneakers and jeans and drinking out of red plastic cups. Craig floats through the crowd, but doesn't see anyone he knows, not even Josh. Above the music—something electronic, nothing he recognizes—he hears a familiar rhythmic *tap tap tap*. Craig shudders: Ping-Pong.

He grabs a beer from the kitchen. For twenty minutes he nurses his drink while pretending to read email on his phone. As he's getting a second beer, Josh approaches from behind.

"Craig, dude. How are you?"

Josh is wearing cargo shorts and a baby blue T-shirt that features a cloud with a postage stamp on it. In his hand is a red plastic cup.

"Josh, hey."

"Great party, huh?"

Craig surveys the room.

"I guess. It's just, who *are* all these people?"

"What do you mean?"

"I don't see any of the coders." Craig tries to remember a few of their names, but the only thing that comes to him is brands of headphones.

"Oh, *them*." Josh sighs. "We had to let them go."

"What? Why?"

"Since the Pillw code's already in place, they weren't needed anymore."

"But there were, like, a dozen of them."

"I told them they could all reapply to Pillw, but, quite frankly, it's a long shot since most of those guys were front end and OS developers, which we don't really need anymore. All that work's already been done by the guys at Pillw. Speaking of which, there's one of them I want you to meet."

Josh calls out across the room.

"Nathan, my man, come here. This is the guy."

A skinny kid wearing jeans and Converse sneakers is having a conversation with a skinny kid wearing jeans and flip-flops. The kid in the flip-flops nods and approaches.

"Hey."

"Nathan, this is Craig, the guy I was telling you about."

"Nice to meet you."

"Craig's an awesome marketer. Did one hell of a job at Seatr. He can't wait to get started with you on Pillw. Isn't that right, Craig?"

"Yup. Can't wait."

"I took a look at a lot of the work you did," Nathan says. "A bit rough, but some good potential. I'm not sure it's entirely scalable, but I think there's enough there to get started."

Someone from across the room catches Nathan's eye. He gives a wave and then turns back to Josh and Craig.

"More on this next week. Take care."

As Nathan walks away, Craig says, "Seems like a nice kid."

"I'm glad you think that. You're now reporting to him."

"*What?*"

Josh's eyes are closed as he shakes his head back and forth.

"I know what you're going to say, Craig."

"Really? What am I going to say, Josh?"

Josh's eyes open.

"Well, then, I guess I *don't* know what you're going to say. Maybe something about his age?"

"It's not that." Craig sighs. "I used to report to you, but you were at least the CEO. You've already built a company. The coders all respected you, I get that. But who's this guy? What's his title?"

"Come on, Craig. You know I'm not into titles."

"I know that, Josh. But what's he going to *do*? Certainly you're into him *doing* something."

"He's going to be in charge of the site. You're running marketing. It just makes sense to have you report to him, okay?"

"So, he's in charge of the site, and I'm in charge of marketing? That means we're equals."

Josh squints.

"Not exactly. You're running marketing, but he's in charge of the entire site so, essentially, you're marketing *his* site. Ergo . . ."

"What is this, rock, paper, scissors?"

"Craig, it's decided."

"He's my boss. That's what you're saying?"

"That's what I'm saying. Anyway, I don't see what *you're* so down about. I have to report to Alex now. You think that makes *me* happy?"

"Alex? Who's Alex?"

Josh motions across the room to where a young woman with tattoos up and down both arms is standing with a can of beer in one hand and an iPhone in the other.

"I told you about her. We slept together last week. And now she's my boss. You don't think that stings?"

In the background, above the music, Craig hears another Ping-Pong game getting started.

"What about James?"

"Huh?"

"James. What about *him*? Was *he* fired?"

"Are you kidding? No way James is leaving. He's a rock star. The board's made him a director."

"Director? So much for not being into titles."

Josh ignores him. As Craig's shaking his head and looking for Ashley—she should be there by now—Josh snaps his fingers.

"I almost forgot. Stay here."

Josh disappears for a second, returning with something big and black and covered in a plastic bag. He hands it to Craig, who fumbles with the plastic, trying to find an opening. He finally just rips it open, pulling out whatever's inside. He feels canvas, sees straps. He's still not sure what it is.

"Backpacks," Josh says. "Cool, huh?"

Craig turns it over and, underneath the Patagonia logo, PILLW is stitched in baby blue letters.

"It was the board's idea. Thought it would be good for morale. Get everybody off on the right foot."

Craig loops the backpack around his left shoulder. It feels good. It's a nice backpack.

"God, these margaritas suck." Josh crushes the red plastic cup and tosses it onto a desk. "I'm going to fire that fucking intern."

Charles and Grace and Roy and Ronnie are finishing up the cheese and crackers. Once they said goodbye to Maddie, and sent her upstairs to watch a movie in her room, they quickly went through a pitcher of martinis and now Charles thinks they're going to run out of gin. He's not sure he has another bottle. Grace clears the small plates, each filled with cracker crumbs and cheese rinds, refusing Ronnie's offer to help.

Charles picks up a small bowl overflowing with olive pits and follows Grace to the kitchen. After they drop off the dishes, Grace pulls a pan of asparagus out of the oven. The smell of garlic fills the room. Charles is about to slice a loaf of French bread when there's a knock at the door. He says, "Who could that be?"

"Well, whoever it is," Grace says, "please get rid of them since dinner will be on the table in less than five minutes."

He nods. Approaching the door, Charles looks through the panes of glass and sees the top of a head that looks familiar. He opens the door.

Randy's standing on the front step wearing faded jeans and a blue button-down shirt with all the buttons off by one.

"You ready to go? Is that what you're wearing?"

Charles looks down at his pink and purple Polo button down, the tails hanging over blue chinos embroidered with green anchors.

"Go? Go where? What are you talking about?"

"Bottlecap, remember?"

Charles just shakes his head.

"*Who*? Oh, that band from the nineties. Is that tonight?"

"Yes, it's tonight, Jesus. Let's go."

"But it's—I didn't get a ticket. Grace and I have guests. We're just sitting down to dinner."

Charles opens the door slightly to give Randy a peek. Just as he does this, Grace begins bringing food out from the kitchen. Some of the smell escapes from the house and is caught by the breeze. Randy's eyes close when he sniffs.

"So I have plans for tonight, okay?"

"But *you* invited *me*. Remember?"

"I'm sorry Randy, it just slipped my mind."

Grace, headed back to the kitchen, clears her throat to get Charles's attention. Charles turns and whispers, "Give me a second." He then steps onto the front steps, closing the door behind him.

"I just thought that," Randy's saying, "after last week, we'd—I don't know—start hanging out again."

"I'm sorry, Randy. We used to be friends but I just—we can't be friends now."

"Why not?"

"Randy, look. We're not the same anymore. We went different ways."

"What, you think you're better than me? Because you're married and you live in Tiger Bay?"

While Randy's saying this, Charles slowly shakes his head back and forth.

"Randy, no. You can be whatever you want to be. It's just, where you are in your life is not where I am in mine."

"And where am I, Charles? Tell me."

"From what I can tell, you still think you're twenty-three. And I hate to break it to you, but you're not."

"Oh, so everyone should just be like you and move out to the suburbs and stick their fucking heads in the sand?"

"Randy, I'm not—I don't have my head in the sand."

He starts to walk away, but stops. Randy turns around.

"Look, you don't want to be friends. That's fine. I mean, it's not fine, but it is what it is. I can't force you. But I need—I lost my job last week."

"Randy, I—I'm sorry to hear that."

"I'm looking for a new job, and I'm filling out a lot of applications. The only problem is, I've got no one to list as a reference. Can I put you?"

"Randy, I don't know. That's usually for people you used to work with. Or who at least know you well."

"I know that, Charles. I'm not an idiot." Randy looks at the ground, then up and down the street. "It's just . . . I don't think anyone I used to work with would vouch for me."

"Randy, I wouldn't—I mean, what would I say? If they called me?"

"My god, Charles, you lie. Is that so hard?" Randy paces in circles on the walkway. "You just say I was prompt, dedicated. Shit like that."

Charles glances into the house through the panes in the door, trying to see what's happening. He sees Grace call their guests to dinner. Roy and Ronnie walk to the dining room with their drinks.

"And where do I tell them I witnessed all this stellar behavior? When we worked on that zine twenty years ago?" Charles wishes he were inside with his wife and their friends, sipping on martinis and talking about their kids. He just wants Randy to leave. "Fine, tell me what I can do. Tell me what I should say if someone calls, and I'll say it."

Randy's head drops and he clasps his hands in front of his chest.

"Thank you, Charles. Thank you. So then, just mention that we're friends. That we talk about work. We—I don't know—we hang out."

"I'll see what I can do. Okay? But I'm not making any promises."

Randy nods eagerly.

"Sure, sure. Wow, Charles, that's great. And listen, this means a lot to me. Really. Anyway, I'll get out of here."

Randy starts walking away. He's almost to his car when he stops and walks back.

"Say, since you're willing to go to bat for me, how about hooking me up with a job at your place?"

"What, Trust?"

"Yeah, sure. Wherever. A job's a job, right?"

Charles hears Grace laugh, and wonders what's making her laugh.

"Randy, I don't know."

"Why not? I mean, how cool would that be? Me and you, working side by side. Just like the old days."

Charles tries to think of something that Randy could do at Trust. The only thing he can think of is the mailroom, but he doubts Randy could even handle that. Charles imagines being called into O'Brien's office and having to defend his recommendation while Tom sits there, shaking his head back and forth.

"Listen, put me down as a reference. If somebody calls, I'll be nice. I promise. But there's no way that—"

"That what, Charles? That you think I'm good enough to work where you work?"

"Randy, it's not that. Really. It's just—"

Randy starts shaking his head in addition to waving his hands.

"You know what? Fuck you."

"Randy, come on. There's no need for—"

"Yes, there is, Charles. You think you're so much better than me, then just fuck right off."

Charles decides he's heard enough. He opens the door and goes into his house. He hears Randy stomp down the driveway and get into his car. It takes two tries before his piece of crap actually starts—Charles can hear the *chug chug chug*—and then Randy finally pulls away. Charles takes a few deep breaths before joining Grace and the Nearys in the dining room. When he sits down, he sees they already have food on their plates. They've been waiting for him.

"Charles," Roy says, "what was that all about?"

Charles is about to say something, but Grace speaks first.

"It's an old friend of his. We had him over for dinner last week."

"He's an idiot," Charles says. "Nothing for us to worry about."

Charles reaches for his glass of wine and takes a sip.

"You should give him a chance." Grace's tone is stern. He hates it when she talks to him like this, especially in front of guests. "People can change."

"No, they can't."

Randy gets on the freeway and heads downtown, toward where Bottlecap's playing. He knows he should head home. He needs to start packing and looking for a new apartment. He also knows from experience that, without a job or reliable source of income, no landlord's going to show him an apartment. That means roommates again, but even they'd need first month's rent and a security deposit, which is money he doesn't have. Randy thinks of his parent's house in Maryland. The spare room and the invitation his mom always makes whenever he goes for a visit. Randy's running out of excuses for saying no.

Passing the mall, he sees Bookstorage. He misses having somewhere to go in the morning. He misses the paycheck.

*Maybe if I go back and talk to Bill he'll give me another chance. I'll offer to work every Saturday for a month for free, just so he knows I'm serious. I'll show up early and work late. I'll do better this time, I swear.*

Randy exits the freeway as a red light appears on his dashboard, the icon of a gas pump blinking on and off. A block away, he spots the club's marquee: BOTTLECAP, ONE NIGHT ONLY, SOLD OUT. He starts to look for parking, but doesn't see any open spaces. As he passes the club, Randy sees a long line of people snaking away from the closed doors.

Down the street, two parking lots display signs that read EVENT PARKING $3. Randy doesn't have three dollars, at least not for parking, so he keeps going. Four blocks down, and one over, he finds a spot. Grabbing the printout of his ticket, and not even bothering to lock the car, he heads toward the club.

Concertgoers approach from all directions. Cars pull up and people jump out to get in line. Randy gauges the crowd. Some are young, some are his age, and a few are even older. There are couples dressed up for a night out, as well as packs of guys out to relive their glory days, drinking beer out of paper bags. He sees lots of T-shirts of bands he used to like, all of them faded. He sees lots of gray hair. He sees heads with no hair at all. He lights a cigarette and goes to the end of the line.

People are smoking, laughing, drinking. Cars go by with loud music blaring out of the open windows. Randy remembers countless nights that began like this. Back then, all he cared about was the moment—having a good time. Now all he can think about is what happens next. Tomorrow. Next week. Each moment serves merely as a stepping stone to the next.

In front of him, a group of three couples are discussing how hard it is to get a decent baby sitter.

"I mean, you'd think we'd be able to find someone who doesn't empty our entire fridge and leave the sink filled with dirty dishes. Or spend the whole night on the couch texting with her boyfriend." The guy's friends are all laughing and shaking their heads in a *that's-so-true* fashion. "Or is that too much to ask for ten dollars an hour?"

Randy's ears prick up.

*Ten dollars an hour?*

It's more than he's ever made in his life. He's about to offer his services when someone approaches from the street, steps onto the sidewalk, and stands behind him. He finishes his cigarette, throws it in the gutter, and sees that a woman has taken his place as the end of the line.

She's wearing a black fitted jacket over an old Bottlecap T-shirt, along with Levi's and open-toed high heel sandals. Randy's wearing Levi's, too, but his don't look anything like hers. Hers fit her long legs snugly, with light lines down the front of the legs from where they've been ironed. Randy's jeans are baggy and stained. He can't remember the last time he washed them. Her hair is long, light brown, and curly. Pink glasses are pushed on top of her head. She checks her phone as people continue to queue up behind her. Randy tries not to be obvious about it, but he's staring. She finally notices.

"Oh, hey."

Caught, Randy knows he needs to say something.

"Hey."

*Haven't lost the touch.*

Mark pulls up in front of the address that appeared on a Post-it a few days ago. It was stuck to the manila folder of clippings in his room. His father had written, *Thought you might be interested* and, below this, *It's never too late.*

The house is big, with white columns, red bricks, and blue shutters. If you squint, it looks like an American flag. There's an SUV in the driveway with a bumper sticker that says MY SON IS AN HONOR STUDENT AT HOLY CROSS ELEMENTARY. Mark leans across the passenger seat and opens the glove box. He takes out a yellowed envelope he put there when he got the rental car two weeks ago. Getting out, he shoves the envelope into his back pocket.

As he walks to the front door, Mark looks down the block and sees similar houses lined up side by side. Even the cars parked in the driveways—SUVs, station wagons, minivans—look the same.

He knocks on the door. She answers.

"Laura. Hi."

She smiles slightly, but then looks uncertain.

"My God. *Mark.*" She glances back inside the house. "What are you doing here?"

"I'm in town. Bottlecap's doing a concert. Tonight. You know, my old band."

She nods. Her brown hair is pulled back into a ponytail. She's wearing jeans and a T-shirt with flowers all over it. Despite some faint wrinkles around her eyes and mouth, Laura looks exactly like she did all those years ago.

"Yeah, I talked to—I saw you on the news."

"Pretty cool, huh?"

"Pretty cool."

"I wasn't sure if you were planning on going to the show, so I thought I'd stop by."

She crosses her arms and pulls them into her chest. She says, "No, Mark. I wasn't planning on going to the show."

He pulls the envelope out of his back pocket and hands it to her.

"Then let me give you this."

"What is it?"

"A letter. From when I lived in Los Angeles. Do you remember? You wrote to me."

"Of course I remember." She laughs. Her laugh is also the same. "I also remember that you never wrote back."

He steps forward and offers her the envelope.

"I did. I just never sent it."

She unfolds her arms and takes it. Turns it over in her hands. The address, written in faded ink, is from twenty years ago. From when she lived across town in a house he spent a lot of time in.

"What—when did you write this?"

"The night before I walked out on the guys. I started it as a letter to them. Telling them why I had to go. Why it was over." Mark's head is down. He's staring at the front steps.

"So why didn't you give it to them?"

"I don't know. I didn't think they'd understand. I didn't really understand it myself."

"But you thought I would?"

"I guess so. Then I chickened out and never sent it. But I always wanted you to have it. To know."

"Even now?"

Mark looks up. He says, "Even now."

She puts the letter in her back pocket, and then shoves her hands into her front pockets.

"You know," Mark says. "I never forgot about you."

"Well, that's a shame. Because I forgot about you."

From inside the house there's a crash, followed by giggles and screams. Laura glances over her shoulder, to inside the house. A male voice tells someone to be careful.

"You have kids?"

She turns and looks at him. He'd forgotten how blue her eyes are.

"Yes. Three."

"What—kind?"

"Kind?" Laura laughs. "Two boys and a girl. My sons are eight. The girl's ten going on forty." She laughs again. Mark doesn't remember her laughing this much when they were together.

*Did we not have fun? Was it really not as good as I remember it?*

Laura looks down. She kicks at the welcome mat.

"Mark, I have to go. And you have to go, too. The show, right?"

A chill comes over Mark. He suddenly remembers. The show. The guys waiting for him. His parents.

Laura gives him a hug. As he holds her, Mark remembers being young and in love with this middle-aged woman who married someone else. She pulls away before he's ready to let go. He tries to hang on, but she twists her shoulders so he reluctantly releases her. She whispers "goodbye," and then turns back to the house. She goes inside, closes the door. Mark can hear Laura's children welcome her, talking excitedly and telling her everything she missed in the few minutes she was gone.

He gets into the rental car and heads for the Dark Star Lounge.

An hour later, Randy's finally thought of something else to say to the woman standing behind him in line.

"I like your shirt."

"Oh, thanks." She looks up from her phone. "I've had it a long time."

"You like the band?"

His voice rises when he asks. He's never met a woman who had his taste in music, let alone who liked Bottlecap.

"They were my first concert. At the Scene. I had to sneak my way in with a fake ID."

"Wow, that's cool. You must have been eight or something, because you sure don't look old now."

She blushes.

"Thanks, but I was fifteen."

The line moves a little, but it's just because people are getting anxious and inching forward. The doors are still closed.

"So, you like Bottlecap?"

"Yeah, I guess," she says. "Or, at least, I did. It was kind of a high school thing. Once I went away to college I stopped listening to them. I think they'd broken up by then anyhow."

"I'm Randy, by the way."

He offers his hand, unsure if it's the right thing to do. But at least it's a move.

"Nice to meet you, Randy. I'm Kat."

She offers her hand and, when Randy touches it, he can't believe how dainty and soft it feels.

"Cat? As in, meow?"

She laughs.

"No, as in Katherine."

Randy nods.

Ahead of them in line, there's some sort of commotion. The conversations suddenly become louder, more animated, news trickling from the front of the line to the back. Randy hears a guy in front of them say, "Finally. The doors are open."

The line begins to move. Kat and Randy shuffle towards the entrance.

"Shit," she says. "I better text my friend again. She has my ticket."

As they walk, Kat frantically tries texting and then calling her friend, except neither works. When they get to the entrance, they step out of line and let people pass them and head into the club. A band's on stage, tuning up, about to go on.

"Goddamn," Kat says. "She probably got hung up. She said she might have some family thing. Well, I guess she had it."

There's desperation in her voice. They stand there for a few seconds, the crowd filing past. Randy hands her his ticket.

"Take mine."

"What? No, I couldn't. We just met and, what about you?"

He shrugs.

"I've seen them a bunch of times. I want you to have it. Really."

She bites her lip. When she does, they get even more red.

"But will—are you sure?"

Randy grins.

"I'm sure."

Kat's about to say something, but doesn't. She just smiles and takes the ticket.

"Thanks."

She leans in for a hug. When Kat does this, he can smell her hair. It smells like apricots. Releasing him, she folds herself back into the line of people entering the club. The first band has started playing, and Randy recognizes the song. It's the Deer Park. He interviewed them twenty years ago in a smelly and beat up van just a few miles from where he's standing. Randy imagines the younger version of himself in the club, moshing in the pit, singing along, having fun. He tries to think of something he could say to that version of himself, something that would prepare for him everything that's going to follow, but he comes up blank.

Randy turns and walks away from the club.


Charles needs more gin. As he wades deeper into the pantry—the room's the size of, and resembles, a small store—the green cap catches the light from the bulb that's still swinging from where he hit it with his head a few seconds ago as he entered the room. He grabs the gin, pulls the string to turn out the light, and reenters the kitchen.

He fills the cocktail shaker halfway with gin. Charles adds a dash of vermouth and walks to the refrigerator to get ice from the door. He puts the top on the cocktail shaker, gives it a good shake, and then grabs the strainer as he enters the den.

"Who's ready for a refill?"

Roy and Ronnie turn and raise their empty glasses. Just as Charles bends over, about to fill Ronnie's glass, there's a knock at the door. It's louder and more insistent than earlier in the evening. Charles frowns, says, "Excuse me," and places the pitcher on the table.

"Charles," Roy says, "you need a hand?"

"Thanks, but no. This'll just take a second."

Charles gets up and marches out of the dining room. He throws open the front door.

"Jesus, Randy, will you just leave me—"

Only it's not Randy. It's Dylan. He has bloodshot eyes and his hands are shaking. Charles sniffs and can smell alcohol.

"Why? Why'd you do it, Charles?"

Charles steps out and quickly closes the door behind him.

"Do what?"

Dylan forces a laugh.

"Don't play dumb with me. Brooks told me you sent him on some wild good chase on Monday, acting all nervous and weird. Later that day I noticed some of my files were missing. On Tuesday I have some strange meeting with O'Brien where he accuses me of all kinds of shit. Then, on Wednesday, I'm fired. Pretty suspicious, don't you think?"

"Look, Dylan, I'm sorry they let you go. Really. But this has nothing to do with me."

Dylan waves his hand, as if casting aside everything that Charles is saying. As he does this, his big silver watch makes a rattling sound.

"Charles, that's bullshit. You know it and I know it."

"Dylan, I'm—I really don't know what you're talking about."

Seconds pass. Charles wishes someone would drive by, or that Grace would come out to check on him. But there's just silence.

"I suppose they gave you the promotion. *My* promotion."

"I'm not sure. Nothing's really—nothing's been decided yet."

"You fucking liar."

"Dylan, look. I'm telling you the truth."

Dylan begins quickly pacing back and forth.

"Jack said you met with Tom on Friday."

"Jack? How does Jack know anything?"

"He's sleeping with Heather. She told him you've been meeting with Tom a lot lately."

*Goddamn Jack.*

"Dylan, that wasn't about you, I swear. Or Sharon. Tom wants me to go to the main office. In Seattle. To talk about next quarter's quotas for the sales guys. That's it."

"You liar. You fucking, goddamn, liar!"

The door opens. Charles turns and sees Grace and Roy. Ronnie's in the background, sipping her martini.

Grace says, "Dylan?" They've met before. Holiday parties. Company barbecues. She and Dylan's wife once organized a company trip to Atlantic City.

Seeing Grace seems to calm Dylan down. He retreats slightly, anger draining from his face. But a second later, it's back.

"Celebrating, are we, Charles? Celebrating my promotion?"

Charles doesn't say anything.

"Honey, what's he talking about?" Grace says this to Charles but she's looking at Dylan.

"Nothing, sweetheart. Dylan's just being—it's sour grapes, that's all."

"Tell her, Charles! The whole fucking office knows. She might as well know, too."

Roy leans in and says, quietly, "Should I call the cops?"

Charles pictures police cars. Flashing sirens. News crews. A story in tomorrow's *Kitty Courier*. He whispers to Roy, "No, don't worry about it. He's just letting off a little steam. It'll be okay."

"Tell them, Charles!" Dylan's fists are curled into tight balls. His voice is practically a scream. "Tell her how you *lied* to O'Brien to get *my* job! Tell them how you fucked me and got me *fired*!"

Dylan's voice echoes in the night. Various lights over various doors turn on, up and down the street. Doors open, people step out to see what's going on. Charles can tell you everyone's name. He knows all his neighbors. And now they know this. Next door, John steps out, onto his porch.

When Dylan speaks again, he's no longer shouting. His voice is actually not much more than a whisper. Beginning to cry, his eyes filled with tears, he says, "Tell them, Charles. Tell them how you ruined my life."

Behind them, there's someone new at the door. Maddie stands in jeans and a T-shirt. She looks at her father.

"Daddy? Is that true?"

Craig finally spots Ashley at the party. He's been texting and calling her for the past two hours, but she hasn't answered. Now he sees her tentatively hovering at the edge of the room, as if unsure she's in the right place.

"You're late."

"Sorry, I got lost."

"Lost? How did you get lost? You've lived here your entire life." Craig takes her by the arm and walks her over to the windows, toward where he used to sit. "We're right off the freeway. How do you miss that?"

Ashley looks out the window, blankly.

"I'm sorry, Craig," she says. "I told you. I was lost."

Out of the corner of his eye, he sees Nathan watching him. Craig fakes a smile and then whispers to Ashley.

"Look, I'm sorry. It's been a rough night. Can we just leave?"

"But we—I just got here. Don't you at least want to show me your office?"

"Sure." He points around the room. "These are the desks. There's the kitchen. We used to have a conference room, but now it's Wimbledon for idiots. It's over there. Now can we go?"

Ashley shrugs, so Craig grabs her hand and leads her through the office. They're almost out the door when Nathan calls out.

"Craig, got a second?"

Leaning in to Ashley, he says, "Meet me in the hallway."

Ashley nods and walks through the door she entered just a few minutes ago.

"Wanted to give you one of these." Nathan hands Craig a pillow. "Thought you should have one of these so you could familiarize yourself with our product. This is next month's selection. Feel how soft it is."

Craig squeezes the pillow. It's indeed soft, but it also feels thin and cheap, like a cotton ball.

"Air, right?" Nathan says. "Doesn't it feel just like *air*?"

*Two weeks ago I was presenting the marketing strategy for an innovative new startup that was going to revolutionize travel. Now I'm sending people air.*

"Wow, yeah—Nathan. This is *awesome*."

Nathan grins. Across the room, Craig sees James grab a beer from the fridge. He's breathing heavily and there's sweat on his forehead. When he catches Craig's eye, he winks.

"I knew you'd like it," Nathan's saying. "So then, see you on Monday? First thing? We're going to crush it."

"Definitely. Crush it."

Craig puts the pillow under his right arm and leaves the office.

He finds Ashley in the hallway staring at the back of her phone. They ride the elevator in silence. Downstairs, people are still arriving for the party. Craig searches for a familiar face, but sees only strangers. They stop by the bike rack and he turns to Ashley.

"I'm sorry about up there. But I'm really glad to see you. *Really* glad. I've been thinking of you every second since the other day. And, well, I'm just glad to be with you again. To be back together."

"Back together?"

"Well, yeah."

He reaches out to take her hand but, when he does, she flinches and his fingers scrape against her wedding band. The diamonds scratch his skin.

"Craig, I can't do this."

Ashley's eyes look dull and her face is washed out.

"Ash, *please*. This can be our chance to get it right."

"Don't call me Ash. And just—get away from me. Right now."

"Why?"

"Craig, *look* at yourself. You look like you're twelve years old and you're heading off to summer camp."

He looks down. He still has the pillow Nathan gave him tucked under his arm and the backpack's slung over a shoulder.

"You dress like you're in the sixth grade and you take a glorified *bus* to work. And, and," she motions to his shoulder. This seems to break her. "You're wearing a fucking *backpack*."

Ashley crumples to the ground. Her purse falls and empties itself onto the concrete. Items scatter—tube of mascara, packet of gum, small tin of Altoids. An amber prescription bottle rolls into the parking lot, coming to a stop under the front tire of a Tesla.

He says, in a whisper, "It's a shuttle."

"Craig, you're going backwards. And I can't—I just don't want to be in that place. Not anymore. Not with you. Not again."

"What, you'd rather go back to Andrew? To *fucking* Andrew?"

"Andrew's good to me. He's better to me than I've been to him." She looks up. "And he's better to me than you ever were."

"That's not true. Stop that."

He kicks at the curb. When he does, the backpack falls off his shoulder. It makes noise as it hits the ground, the metallic buckles and clasps clanging on the concrete. Craig grabs the backpack and throws it across the parking lot. It bounces off a black Chevy Volt.

"Ash, please. I'm *begging* you."

"You ruined me once, Craig. I won't let you do it again."

"For god's sake, stop blaming me for what happened. It wasn't my fault."

"What we did was wrong, Craig. In Charlottesville. It was *wrong*."

"Don't bring that up."

"We could have been parents. We could have had a child. We could have had something to love."

"I loved you."

"Loved me? You didn't even *like* me." Ashley begins picking up the things that fell out of her purse. But rather than put them back in, she throws them into the parking lot. Slowly, one at a time. The gum. A packet of tissues. Her checkbook.

Craig moves toward her, grabbing the upper part of her right arm. When he tries to get her to stand up, she lets out a small scream so he lets go. A young couple heading into the building throws them glances.

"There's no need to create a scene, Ashley. Jesus."

"You made me do it, Craig. You *made* me."

"I didn't *make* you. Stop saying that. We made the decision to-gether. You're rewriting history."

Craig looks up at the building, to the window in Seatr's office that overlooks the parking lot. He sees figures, skinny silhouettes holding cups and beer bottles. He sees fingers pointing.

Ashley stands up, grabs her purse, and stumbles toward him. Craig backs up, not sure what she's going to do.

"I would *love* to rewrite history, Craig. I would write it so that I never married Andrew. Or took my stupid job." She's speaking slowly and staring at the freeway. "And I'd go even further than that. To that day in the bookstore. When I first met you."

She focuses for a second on Craig, but then turns toward the parking lot. She says, "If I could rewrite history, Craig, I'd write you right out." And then she walks away.

He considers going after her, but doesn't. Instead, he sits down on the curb inside of the semicircle of stuff that fell out of her purse. He grabs the pillow and pulls it in, close to his chest. He buries his head. The sounds all around him are muffled.

A few minutes later, he registers someone walk up beside him and stop.

"Ashley?"

He looks up and sees James. Behind him stand Josh, Nathan, Alex, and a few other people he recognizes from the party.

"Come back upstairs," James says. "Let's play some Ping-Pong."

When he doesn't move, James bends down and stretches out his arms, offering to help Craig up. That's when he notices the tattoos. Two four letter words, one on each of James's hands, a letter on each knuckle: GAME OVER.

Ashley turns into the driveway, pulling up alongside Andrew's Audi. She glares at the garage door. The garage filled with all the useless crap they never use and don't want. She revs the engine and releases the brakes, launching the car forward. It strikes the garage door with a dull crash. The impact throws up a cloud of dust, paint chips rain down. Airbags deploy and feel soft against her cheek. It makes her want to close her eyes and rest. But then she thinks of Craig and his pillow. The backpack. All the mistakes she's made in the past two weeks.

The garage door falls apart in three sheets of plywood. She'd wanted there to be a hole shaped like her car, like you see in cartoons, but instead the whole thing's come down in pieces. Andrew appears at the back of the garage, standing at the door that leads from the garage into the house. He's silhouetted by light from the kitchen. She gets out of the car.

"Ashley, what are you doing?" There's panic in his voice. "Are you okay? Did you lose control?"

Her own voice, when she speaks, is even and calm.

"Yes, Andrew. I lost control."

She looks at the front of her Prius. It doesn't look dented, but the hood is scratched and something inside the car is chiming, asking for her attention. The door's still open so maybe it's that. She looks around at all the stuff in the garage. The stacks. The piles. The mountains of junk.

Neighbors told them to keep a pair of old mattresses. You never know when you're going to need them. Her parents said they shouldn't throw out their old microwave. It might come in handy someday. She begged Andrew to get rid of his books, but he swore he'd reread them. Every time they were going to toss something, they held on to it. Just in case.

*All our lives we were taking the wrong advice, listening to the wrong voices.*

Cars go by, slowing, gawking, jaws dropped. She doesn't care anymore.

"Ashley!" Andrew grabs her by the shoulders. "Talk to me. What happened?"

"I just wanted—I just wanted—"

"What, Ashley, what?"

"I just wanted to park in the garage. For once."

His look softens—less scared, more understanding—and he pulls her close. For a few minutes they don't speak.

Finally, Ashley, "Why did we wait, Andrew?"

When he doesn't answer, she asks again, "Why did we make that decision over another?"

"I don't know, darling." Now his own voice is calm. It's not much louder than the chiming still coming out of the car. "I really don't. But does it matter now? The decision was made."

"We can do something about it."

"We can't Ash—Ashley, we can't. Too much time's gone by."

He lets go of her and she sits down on a stack of old magazines. She's flanked by an assortment of paint cans on one side and a belt sander on the other that Andrew bought two years ago but has never used.

"We can do *something*," she says.

"We looked into that, sweetheart. That clinic out west. It costs a fortune. We don't have a fortune."

"Andrew, *please*. We need to do something."

He's about to speak, but doesn't. So she does.

"Andrew, we need to change. I just feel like we haven't changed, that's all."

He finally says, "Okay, Ashley. We'll change."

She looks up at him and smiles. He reaches down and helps her up, the stack of magazines falls over when she stands. He leads her toward the door off the kitchen.

Going back into the house, and just to see what happens, Andrew presses the button to open the garage. What remains of the door falls to the ground, dust and chips of old flaking paint make clouds that are lit up by the streetlight two doors down. The engine pulls and the chain makes all its usual noise. Something's missing, but it still works.

Mark's ears are ringing. It's nearly midnight, the night having gone by in a blur. The club's emptying out, more people are backstage than lingering on Dark Star's huge floor or at the bar. Gary's in the corner with Dave, smiles on both their faces. Gary's covered in sweat and still breathing hard from the show. Steve's with his wife and older brother, Phil. Mark remembers Phil from back in the day. He used to look scary with piercings and long hair. Now, with his hair thinned and silver, he looks like a banker or a lawyer. The other bands are back here too, along with their friends and relatives. People are drinking beer and chugging cocktails out of red plastic cups. Someone even sneaks hits off a joint from a cupped hand. The mood is festive and celebratory.

Mark can't believe it's over. All those weeks of preparation. The months spent agonizing over whether or not to make the trip. The anxiety. The questions. Would people show up? Would he be able to get on stage and play if they did? All of that now fades away. It's done. Mark feels deflated. Curiously empty.

He thinks about his life in Manhattan, his apartment and job. They seem as distant to him now as that life would have seemed when he lived here, when he could only imagine what it would be like to be the age he is now. He thinks of his co-workers, his neighbors. The place where he gets bagels, the pizza joint on the corner he can see from his living room. Somehow he doesn't believe that life belongs to him. That that's where he ended up.

Finally, he spots them. His parents look out of place among the sweaty rockers and middle-aged well-wishers. After he waves at them from across the room, they begin to make their way through the boisterous crowd.

His mom reaches him first. She gives him a big hug and a kiss. She says something, but it's lost in the noise of the room. His dad is next. They hug. His father feels like bones in a suit. He pats his back and pulls away, looking into Mark's eyes. They're his eyes. He says one word, tears forming.

"Son."

www.ingramcontent.com/pod-product-compliance
Lightning Source LLC
Chambersburg PA
CBHW020639180626
46816CB00003B/1042